TELL ME TO RUN

CHARLOTTE BYRD

Identifiers

ISBN (e-book): 978-1-63225-059-9

ISBN (paperback): 978-1-63225-060-5

ISBN (hardcover):978-1-63225-061-2

❀ Created with Vellum

ABOUT TELL ME TO RUN

From the moment we met, Nicholas Crawford has been an enigma.

He's a man with an unknown past and a mysterious future.

He's a criminal, a liar, a mastermind, and the love of my life.

I became a criminal for him.

I rescued him and now it's his turn to do something for me.

When I discover that everything I believed about my family is a lie, I need his help to uncover the truth.

Who am I ?

Where do I come from?

Why is there so much deceit?

I'm in a dark place, and I'm all alone, and he is the only person who can pull me out of it.

He is my only hope, what happens if that's not enough?

Decadent and delicious 4th book of the new and addictive Tell Me series by bestselling author Charlotte Byrd.

PRAISE FOR CHARLOTTE BYRD

"BEST AUTHOR YET! Charlotte has done it again! There is a reason she is an amazing author and she continues to prove it! I was definitely not disappointed in this series!!"
★★★★★

"LOVE!!! I loved this book and the whole series!!! I just wish it didn't have to end. I am definitely a fan for life!!! ★★★★★

"Extremely captivating, sexy, steamy, intriguing, and intense!" ★★★★★

"Addictive and impossible to put down."
★★★★★

"What a magnificent story from the 1st book through book 6 it never slowed down always surprising the reader in one way or the other. Nicholas and Olive's paths crossed in a most unorthodox way and that's how their story begins it's exhilarating with that nail biting suspense that keeps you riding on the edge the whole series. You'll love it!" ★★★★★

"What is Love Worth. This is a great epic ending to this series. Nicholas and Olive have a deep connection and the mystery surrounding the deaths of the people he is accused of murdering is to be read. Olive is one strong woman with deep convictions. The twists, angst, confusion is all put together to make this worthwhile read." ★★★★★

"Fast-paced romantic suspense filled with twists and turns, danger, betrayal, and so much more." ★★★★★

"Decadent, delicious, & dangerously addictive!" - Amazon Review ★★★★★

"Titillation so masterfully woven, no reader can resist its pull. A MUST-BUY!" - Bobbi Koe, Amazon Review ★★★★★

"Captivating!" - Crystal Jones, Amazon Review ★★★★★

WANT TO BE THE FIRST TO KNOW ABOUT MY UPCOMING SALES, NEW RELEASES AND EXCLUSIVE GIVEAWAYS?

Sign up for my newsletter: https://www.subscribepage.com/byrdVIPList

Join my Facebook Group: https://www.facebook.com/groups/276340079439433/

Bonus Points: Follow me on BookBub and Goodreads!

ABOUT CHARLOTTE BYRD

Charlotte Byrd is the bestselling author of romantic suspense novels. She has sold over 1 Million books and has been translated into five languages.

She lives near Palm Springs, California with her husband, son, a toy Australian Shepherd and a Ragdoll cat. Charlotte is addicted to books and Netflix and she loves hot weather and crystal blue water.

Write her here:

charlotte@charlotte-byrd.com

Check out her books here:

www.charlotte-byrd.com

Connect with her here:

www.facebook.com/charlottebyrdbooks

www.instagram.com/charlottebyrdbooks

www.twitter.com/byrdauthor

Sign up for my newsletter: https://www.subscribepage.com/byrdVIPList

Join my Facebook Group: https://www.facebook.com/groups/276340079439433/

Bonus Points: Follow me on BookBub and Goodreads!

facebook.com/charlottebyrdbooks

twitter.com/byrdauthor

instagram.com/charlottebyrdbooks

bookbub.com/profile/charlotte-byrd

ALSO BY CHARLOTTE BYRD

All books are available at ALL major retailers! If you can't find it, please email me at charlotte@charlotte-byrd.com

The Perfect Stranger Series
The Perfect Stranger
The Perfect Cover
The Perfect Lie
The Perfect Life
The Perfect Getaway

All the Lies Series
All the Lies
All the Secrets
All the Doubts

Tell me Series

Tell Me to Stop

Tell Me to Go

Tell Me to Stay

Tell Me to Run

Tell Me to Fight

Tell Me to Lie

Wedlocked Trilogy

Dangerous Engagement

Lethal Wedding

Fatal Wedding

Tangled Series

Tangled up in Ice

Tangled up in Pain

Tangled up in Lace

Tangled up in Hate

Tangled up in Love

Black Series

Black Edge

Black Rules

Black Bounds

Black Contract

Black Limit

Not into you Duet

Not into you

Still not into you

Lavish Trilogy

Lavish Lies

Lavish Betrayal

Lavish Obsession

Standalone Novels

Dressing Mr. Dalton

Debt

Offer

Unknown

1

OLIVE

"*I*t is possible to have sex with more than one person at the same time even though it is not possible to love more than one person at one time."

This is what Sydney says when I ask her to tell me what is going on in her life.

We are sitting in the waiting room with our legs crossed facing each other. I am holding a small paper cup filled with black coffee that she bought me from the vending machine.

Two gulps later, all of the liquid is gone and my tongue is on fire.

She wants to talk about Owen and his

medical condition.

She wants to hold my hand and hold me while I cry.

But I want her to tell me about all of the people that she and James have slept with over the last two months.

I've spent almost five days here, breathing the stale recycled air and walking up and down the polished squeaky floors.

I know almost all of the nurses by name and the shifts that they tend to work. I know how many kids they have and how many men have disappointed them.

Time passes slowly here on the fourth floor and when bursts of excitement do occur, they are not particularly life-affirming.

Nicholas doesn't think that I should spend so much time here, even though he stops short of actually telling me this.

My mother, on the other hand, doesn't. She has visited Owen twice since he fell into the coma and each visit was only an hour or so.

When I ask her why she doesn't stay longer, she says that she'll come back if his condition changes but she has her own life to lead.

"*If* his condition changes."

She doesn't even do me the courtesy of saying *when.*

That's just another lie, of course. We both know that there is nothing much really to do besides lie in her recliner and watch hours of television while smoking.

Given that the chairs here have straight backs and thin padding and there are no-smoking signs everywhere, Owen should probably consider himself lucky that she has visited the few times that she has.

"Are you sure you want me to talk about this?" Sydney asks, shifting her weight from one side of the chair to another.

She has always enjoyed food and the body that came with that indulgence, but during her time in Hawaii, she seemed to have gained a few pounds.

"Your breasts look...bigger, if that's even possible," I point out.

Her eyes light up. "Yeah, they are. I gained some weight and luckily it seemed to all go to my chest."

"I bet James likes that." I smile.

"He likes everything about this," she says, running her index finger up and down her curves. "Can't get enough."

I have known Sydney long enough to remember when she struggled with accepting herself.

There were many crash diets, five-day water fasts, and hours at the gym. All of this effort produced only temporary results.

While I admire the woman that she has become, I would be lying if I didn't admit that I was also more than a little bit jealous.

Though I am only a little bit overweight according to the dreadful body-mass index scale, I hate every roll and curve.

I want to look perfect even though I know that there is no such thing. I want to look toned and fit and with a small waist. I want to have the kind of body that I think Nicholas deserves (even though he is more than happy with the one I have).

This is my dirty little secret, the one no one knows except me. No one, not even Sydney, who knows everything.

I dig my fingers into the packet of salty potato chips and shove a handful into my mouth.

When I lick my fingers dry of all of the crumbs, I nod for her to continue.

"We don't have to talk about this," she whispers, looking around.

The waiting room is deserted and there is less than a foot of space between us.

"I'd like to hear more because it's...distracting me and I need some distraction. But if you don't want to share, that's fine."

Her eyes light up when she leans closer to me. "I've never experienced anything like this before," she says, licking her lips.

"What do you mean?"

"Well, with my ex...he wasn't into anything like this, he was quite conservative in the bedroom. So, after we broke up, I went to some of these clubs by myself. But doing this with a man I love...it's just...there is nothing like it."

She twirls her hair and looks up at the ceiling like a lovesick schoolgirl.

"What kind of stuff have you done?" I ask.

She takes a deep breath before giving me all of the details.

They have fooled around with two sets of couples and then with two couples at once.

They have fooled around with a single woman who only wanted to be with her.

She has been with two men at once, one of them being James.

"What do you like best?" I ask.

"It's a different experience every time. People are different. There are different levels of physical and emotional chemistry. I like this one couple we met a few times but it's also because we got to know them quite well. We went out to dinner, clubbing, that kind of thing."

"And doing all of this, it doesn't have a bad impact on your relationship? I mean, is there jealousy, or resentment, or anything like that?"

"Nope." Sydney shakes her head. "I thought that maybe there would be at first, but since we were into this right from the beginning, I think that's what helped us avoid all of that."

"But you always do it together? You are always both in the room when it happens?" I ask.

"Yes." She nods. "That's the only rule. We both have to be there."

2

OLIVE
WHEN I SEE HIM...

I don't expect Sydney to stay more than a few hours but she refuses to leave without me. We curl up in those light pink chairs with the spindly legs and talk for hours as if we were back in college.

A nurse brings us blankets to keep us warm and gives us the remote to change the channel, but we just turn the television off and bury our heads in her phone watching our favorite funny YouTube videos.

It doesn't take long for me to relax and actually forget why we're both here.

Finally, around one o'clock in the morning, after yet another coffee and Red Bull run, Sydney asks me to take her to see Owen.

"Only if you promise to go home," I say.

"I'll only go home when you do."

I smile and give her a nod.

"Are you actually planning on sleeping here?"

"I don't know," I admit.

I have already spent a few nights in those chairs before and they were not at all restful.

"You need some real sleep, Olive. You're not doing anyone any good running yourself ragged like this."

She's right, of course. I need to take care of myself so that I can be there for Owen.

"I'm just...afraid of leaving him," I say.

This is the first time I have admitted this fear out loud and it sends shivers down my body.

She waits for me to explain.

I go into as much detail about the shooting as I can before I start to feel physically sick and have to turn away from her.

"It's going to be okay," she says even though we both know it's a lie.

I would like to believe her, but all signs are pointing to the fact that it won't be.

There are very bad men who want my brother dead and nothing is going to stop them until they kill him.

"I don't think he's safe here," I finally say. "Alone in this room. There are no guards and anyone can come up here and...finish the job."

My voice cracks at the thought.

Of course, I know that there is not much I can do to stop them if they do come, but just being here makes me feel like I'm preventing something from happening.

"What does Nicholas think about this?" Sydney asks.

I shrug and look away.

My presence here has been the source of more than a few arguments.

He knows that someone is after Owen and that's why he wants me to stay as far away as possible from this place.

He doesn't seem to grasp the fact that he's my brother and I love him.

I am all he has and he is the only family I have.

"You have Nicholas, though," Sydney points out. "He loves you and that's why he doesn't want you to be here."

I shrug and look down at the floor.

"What? What's wrong?" she asks.

"I don't know if that's true," I admit.

"What do you mean?"

I didn't want to get into this tonight, but since she is here and we haven't spoken for what feels like a million years, the words just come spilling out.

"I am not sure if he loves me because we haven't said that to each other yet," I say.

She shakes her head.

She knows about my issue with that word.

She knows how hard it is for me to say it, but she has expected that Nicholas would be the one to take the initiative.

He would be the one to tell me how he feels and that would force me to admit my own feelings for him.

But much to my disappointment, none of that has happened.

"He must love you," she says under her breath. "He just might have the same kind of hang-up you do."

"What are the chances of that?" I ask, rolling my eyes. "What are the chances that we are just two people who are emotionally stunted as opposed to two people who like each other but don't really love one another?"

"Don't say that," she says. "You love him. I know you do."

I touch my knuckles with my index finger.

She's right.

I do love him.

And that's what hurts so much. I can't bring myself to say the words out loud, especially since he is not doing it first.

Not long ago, I thought that I could just force myself to do it once I heard him say it.

But now...it has been a while and he hasn't said anything.

And the more time that passes the more I think that maybe he doesn't love me at all.

"He's worried about you, Olive. He doesn't want you to be here in case something worse happens to Owen."

When our eyes meet, I wonder how she cannot understand what it is that I'm going through?

Doesn't she see that *that's* exactly *why* I have to be here?

Owen is my brother and I need to do everything in my power to protect him.

Even though there isn't much I can do.

Even if it seems pointless.

I have to be here because I will never forgive myself for not being here if something were to happen.

"Tell me more about what your mom said," Sydney insists. "About how he's not really your brother."

I bite my lip.

I don't even know where to begin.

"She just came here and dropped this bomb in my lap," I repeat what I told her earlier.

Even though I have said these words before, they feel just as foreign now as they did earlier.

According to her, Owen is not my brother.

According to her, she is not my mother.

The only family I had is now gone.

Yet, when I think about them, they are still there.

I can't think of them as anything but my mother and brother. Without them, I'm lost like an untethered astronaut tumbling through space.

I get up to get another cup of coffee from the vending machine. That's when I see him.

3

OLIVE

WHEN I SEEK THE TRUTH…

*H*e walks into the room with his shoulders broad and his eyes searching for mine. When he sees me, he rushes over, wrapping his arms around my shoulders and overwhelming me with a strong aroma of cinnamon.

My mouth starts to water even before he pulls out a bag of pastries from his satchel.

"Oh my God, these smell delicious," I say, licking my lips.

I reach for it to peek inside but Nicholas takes it away from me.

"You can only have one if you promise to go home and get some rest," he says sternly.

I tilt my head to one side.

I'm about to protest but Sydney grabs the bag out of my hand and starts to pull me away from him.

"What are you doing?" I ask.

My feet make it a few steps toward the door before I realize what I'm doing.

There is nothing else I yearn for more in this world than to climb into my bed and get some uninterrupted sleep, but I can't leave Owen alone.

"No, I can't." I push her away.

"That's why I'm here," Nicholas says. "That's why I brought my laptop. I have some work to catch up on and I'll stay out here for as long as it takes."

I continue to put up a fight, but the conversation is pretty much over.

Nicholas has made his case and, with my eyes getting heavy and my shoulders slouching down, my body is shutting down.

Sydney and I take a ride share back and arrive at our place fifteen minutes later.

We head straight to our bedrooms but not before I blurt out what my mother told me about Owen.

"He's in love with you?" Sydney asks. "How does she even know?"

"He told her. He was drunk and high and they were talking about life and it just came out."

I don't know how else to explain it.

That's all I know.

It's all I can ever know until he wakes up.

"Do you think she's telling you the truth?" Sydney asks.

This question has ping-ponged back and forth in my mind for some time now.

My mother has lied about a great many things and I wouldn't put anything past her.

"Maybe," I finally say with a shrug. "Perhaps it's just a sick game that she's playing. I don't know."

"Then you should get a DNA test," Sydney says.

We leave it at that and say goodnight.

I am so tired that I fall asleep quickly but the night isn't restful.

I toss and turn, waking up every few hours.

Every time I open my eyes, the same thought pops into my mind: How soon can I get that DNA test done?

————

THE NEXT FEW weeks are a blur just like the previous.

I spend my days oscillating between waiting for Owen to wake up and waiting for someone to come here and finish the job.

Neither happen, leaving me in a state of purgatory.

Luckily, Nicholas, Sydney, and James are kind enough to take some of the burden off my shoulders.

James is in town visiting with Sydney, and even he insists on taking a few overnight shifts, even though I insist that it's not necessary.

I hate to admit it but it's nice to be back in Boston again. I feel like I have some semblance of my old life back only I don't have to go to my dreadful job.

The money situation still bothers me, but Nicholas' check has cleared and the second one did as well so I put my suspicions out of my mind for now.

I have enough to worry about and can't get myself bogged down with all of the unknowns in my life.

As days turn into weeks, we develop a schedule that seems to suit everybody.

Nicholas gives up his hotel room and temporarily moves in with me.

I say *move in* because he doesn't have a date by which he plans on leaving.

He was going to get another hotel suite but I insist that he stay in my two-bedroom along with James. After a few days, the whole arrangement feels a lot like college.

James had a lot of vacation days and he is using them to visit Sydney as they try to figure out what they are going to do about their relationship.

He asked her to marry him and she said yes, but they haven't told her mother yet.

She doesn't even know about Sydney having a boyfriend, so when she comes for her visit tomorrow there are going to be a lot of bombs dropped in her lap.

At first, Nicholas and James weren't sure about staying with us in our apartment, but both Sydney and I insisted and it became something of an extended slumber party.

Usually, we have dinners together at the hospital where Sydney meets me after work and one of the guys takes the evening shift to give me some rest.

It feels good to have people in my life who care about me and what I'm going through. They are supportive and understanding and really there.

That's something that I haven't ever really had growing up.

And that's exactly what makes me feel so shitty about keeping this secret.

I told Nicholas and later James what my mother revealed to me about my lineage. I cried to Nicholas about it many nights trying to figure out what it all means if the woman I think is my mother is really not and the man I think is my brother is really not.

I've gotten so used to defining myself in opposition to this family that I grew up in (especially, my parents) that now I find myself completely lost as to who I really am.

If I'm not their daughter then whose daughter am I?

When I talk to Nicholas about this for what feels like the millionth time, he brings up an interesting point.

"Maybe this is your chance for a do-over," he says. "You've had a pretty shitty family, no offense-"

"No offense taken," I say, raising my hands.

"Well, maybe you should try to find out who your real family is. Maybe you'll surprise yourself."

4

OLIVE
WHEN I GO BACK AND FORTH...

*N*icholas has a nice spin on the situation.

I mean, at least my biological mother never tried to pretend that she was taken hostage in order to get me to pay her debts.

Anyone would be better than that, right?

But what if she's not?

What if she's bad in her own way?

She did give me up for adoption to that woman, how great could she be?

Nicholas doesn't have an answer or even a suggestion so he just wraps his arms around me and holds me tightly.

I wait for him to say that he loves me, but he doesn't.

Anger starts to rise within me, but I push it away.

Why are you getting so mad? I ask myself. It's not like you're out there saying that shit to him either.

It's at this point that I want to tell him what I haven't yet.

I want to tell him the truth about Owen.

There's a man who loves me in every way that you don't, or at least, you won't say that you do.

I especially want to say these things to him when I've had a few drinks. But I bite my tongue.

I don't know if any of it is true.

My mother is a pathological liar.

She lies for no reason whatsoever.

She lies just to stir things up and make herself feel better.

I can't know if I can believe anything she told me until he wakes up.

And even if it is...what does that mean?

Do I love him like *that*?

Do I even like him in any romantic way?

No. I don't. Right?

Whenever my mind starts to swim, I turn to Sydney and ask her how much longer do I need to wait? She doesn't have any more information than I do and tells me to do what I already know I need to do.

"Go check the post office box," she says with a shrug.

"I can't," I say, shaking my head.

"You say that every day. What's the big deal about checking the mail?"

"Because if the results aren't there then I have to wait another day, at the very least. And if they are then...then I have to open the envelope and find out the truth."

Sydney laughs and rolls her eyes. "I bet you were this exact same way when you were waiting on acceptance letters from school."

"Of course, I was," I say, tilting my head annoyed. "What other way is there to be?"

"You could accept the certainty that what has happened already happened," she says. "And opening the letter and finding out the results isn't going to change that one way or another."

I cross my arms and open my mouth to say something smart in return but nothing comes out.

"Yeah...you know I'm right!"

"If I could do that then I'd be a lot more enlightened than I am right now and you and I both know that that's not going to happen any time soon," I mumble.

———

SYDNEY IS the only one who knows what my mother told me about Owen. She's the only one who knows that he may be in love with me. I don't know how that's related to the results of the DNA test but that seems to make the stakes higher somehow.

I walk downstairs where the row of post office boxes line up against the wall near the front door.

The mail woman is still there.

I had wanted to wait long enough for her to leave but for the fourth day in a row, I catch her mid-sorting.

"You waiting for something important?" she asks with a casual smile on her face.

She is in her fifties and one of those women who wears her gray hair proudly.

Her ears are adorned with thick door knockers and her government-issued uniform is taut against her large breasts.

"Um..." I start to say, debating whether or not I should lie. "Yes."

There is no use in obfuscating the truth when the only reason I'm watching her do her job every day is because I am clearly anticipating something.

She smiles knowingly.

I hold my breath as I wait for her to ask me to explain but she doesn't.

She's a professional. Her job is to deliver the mail, not snoop around about its contents.

I wait for her to sort the mail in my neighbors' boxes, pretending like I am even slightly interested in the potluck the neighbors are putting together or the condo association monthly meeting that's going to be held on Thursday.

Finally, it's my turn.

She organizes the mail in her cart and then hands me all of mine as one big packet.

"Good luck," she says, turning toward the door.

I wait until she disappears outside before frantically going through it.

Suddenly, there it is!

I was half expecting a large package but the letter is normal sized with what looks to be one sheet of paper.

The only reason I know that it's from them is that the DNAPlus logo is right there in the top left hand corner of the envelope.

For a second, I consider running up the stairs and opening it in my room, but I know that as soon as I walk over the threshold, Sydney will want to know if it came.

No, it's best to open it here.

I take a deep breath.

It's going to be okay, I say to myself. Either way, it's going to be fine.

Either she's my mother or she's not.

Either he's my brother or he's not.

It's not going to change anything.

I open the envelope feverishly, nearly ripping the whole thing in half.

When I unfold the letter, my hands are trembling.

I skim the bullshit at the beginning and search for the results. They are at the bottom.

I read the results over and over again to make sure that I didn't make a mistake. Then I read the fine print.

My mother was not lying.

She's not my biological mother and Owen is not my biological brother. That's with 100% certainty.

When my head stops buzzing, I sit down on the steps and read the letter again.

Again.

And again.

A part of me is hoping for the results to be different.

Another part is excited by the prospect of finding another family.

A part of me is terrified of what I might find.

"Is that it?" Sydney walks up to me from behind.

I guess I've been gone a bit too long and she noticed.

I hand her the letter without saying a word.

"How do you feel about this?"

"I have no idea."

"What are you going to do?"

I shrug.

"Are you going to look for your real mom?"

"Yes." I nod.

I don't know how I feel about Owen.

I don't know how I feel about my mom not being my biological mom but the one thing I know for sure is that I'm going to look for her now.

"Who do you think she could be?" Sydney asks.

I want her to be someone kind and fabulous and effervescent, someone completely the opposite of my real mother.

But I'm also a realist.

People don't just give up their kids for no reason.

Maybe she was, or is a drug addict.

Maybe she was a teenager who couldn't take care of a baby.

Maybe she was abused or even raped.

Or maybe she just didn't want me.

"What about Owen?" Sydney asks. "I guess he knew this all along."

"He's my brother whatever this piece of paper says. I love him like a brother and I always will. And I'm also pissed at him. I'm mad as hell. He should not have kept this from me. He should *not* have kept *her* secret."

5

OLIVE

WHEN SHE COMES TO VISIT...

I have never seen Sydney freak out like this before.

She hasn't seen her mother in almost six months. She always lost her head a little bit whenever she came to town but this was taking it to a whole new level.

The main thing that changed was the frantic energy that suddenly consumed the whole place.

Sydney is usually calm and collected and pretty easygoing but whenever her mother is even in the vicinity of this continent, she starts to clean and pack and generally buzz around like a bee.

This time, however, with James here, Sydney is not only cleaning her room, the living room, and the kitchen but also behind the stove and deep in the cupboards.

"Is she really going to look there?" I ask.

"She doesn't find anything out here then, yes, she will," Sydney says, nodding her head.

When she dusts every last inch of the living room, and by that I mean every last inch including the inside of the lamp shades and the crown molding, Sydney mops and shines the floors until you can eat off them.

"I don't think we should walk on them until she shows up," I say jokingly.

"You've read my mind," she agrees, completely serious.

I sigh loudly with annoyance but don't say another word.

I know that she's only doing this to make herself feel better. It gives her a sense of control in a world where she has none.

She doesn't know how her mother will react to James and she knows that every part of her will be carefully inspected and scrutinized.

Sydney works hard for two full days and spends the last few hours before her mother's arrival obsessing over which outfits they should wear.

James is a lot less concerned about the meeting and this seems to stress Sydney out even more.

I hear them arguing through the closed door.

When they come back out, James is still wearing the same thing he wore earlier, a dress shirt with jeans and a blazer.

He has stood his ground but his confidence has taken quite a blow.

"Are you sure you don't want me to leave?" I ask again.

I don't really want to be here but I will stay if she needs me to. The way she looks at me with her eyes all big and wide, I know that I have no other choice.

I have to stay.

Sydney's mother arrives right after seven.

Dressed in an elegant black suit and four-inch stilettos, she does not look a bit like a woman who just spent more than twenty hours on an international flight.

Her hair is pulled up into a bun and her hands are small, but strong.

Having attended the best schools along with Cambridge University, she speaks flawless English with a posh British accent and insists that James call her by her first name, Hilary.

I have met Hilary a few times before and she welcomes me with a warm hug like an old friend.

Her manners are impeccable yet there is a distance between us.

When I first met her, I foolishly thought that maybe she would think of me as more than just her daughter's friend and roommate.

She was kind and cordial and I mistook that to mean that she wanted to be my friend, or even a mother figure.

But after a few more visits, I realized that her manners are deceptive. She makes everyone feel like they are a close friend but that doesn't mean that it's true.

For some reason I expect her to be cool and harsh with James, but she is, again, very pleasant and nice.

I don't know her well enough to read her but when I help Sydney with the wine, I get the sense that it's not going as well as I thought.

"She seems to really like me," James says, throwing his arm around Sydney's shoulder when Hilary excuses herself and uses the bathroom.

Sydney stares at him with her mouth dropping open.

"What? She likes me, right?" He looks at us innocently.

I can't help but laugh.

"She doesn't?" he asks, his eyebrows raising to the middle of his forehead. "Wait, what? No, she does. She's acting so...nice."

"That's what she does," Sydney says.

"No, she's not being fake nice, she's being really...kind," James insists.

But Sydney just shakes her head.

Leaning her head on his shoulder and looking up at his beautiful tan face, she whispers something comforting into his ear.

Hilary doesn't stay long.

She says that she's tired and needs some rest, which is of course understandable.

But she does expect to see Sydney for brunch tomorrow at the Ritz. Sydney straightens her back and forces a smile. After a few hugs and best wishes, she calls a ride share and leaves.

As soon as the door closes, Sydney gives out a big sigh of relief. James rubs her shoulders as she kneels down and takes off her heels.

"See, it all went well," James insists. "She likes me. How could she not?"

Sydney glares at him.

"Syd, I'm a doctor. I have an MD. I work with sick kids. I am quite easy on the eyes. And I love you. What kind of mother wouldn't want me for a son-in-law?"

"He does have a point," I agree.

"You two have no idea what you're talking about," she says, shaking her head as she lets her hair down out of its tight braid. "Tomorrow is when I get to hear all the truth about what my mother really thinks about you. Tomorrow is when she is really going to lay it all on me."

She unclasps her bra in the back and pulls it out through her shirt, letting out a sigh of relief once her breasts are free.

I yearn to do the same thing but with James here I decide against it.

Glancing out of the window, I see Hilary climbing into the car that she ordered.

That's my cue.

I go into my room and change into the most comfortable pair of sweats, joggers and a loose t-shirt along with a hoodie. I make sure to take off my bra and zip the hoodie up so that it's not obvious that I'm not wearing one.

"Okay, I'm going to go and relieve Nicholas at the hospital," I say.

6

OLIVE
WHEN I MEET WITH HIM…

I wait for him to say *I love you* first.

I should be able to say it first. I should be stronger than that, but for some reason I can't.

Times like these should bring people together.

They should force them to focus on what's really right.

Isn't that so? Isn't that what all of those TV shows and books teach us about life?

Whenever something significant happens, something as big as what happened to Owen, that's when everything becomes clearer.

That's when people realize that those feelings they've had for someone, they actually mean something.

That's when people decide to move in together.

That's when people decide to get engaged.

Maybe even get married.

I'm not saying that's what I want from Nicholas.

I am definitely not waiting for a marriage proposal.

But sitting here across from him in this uncomfortable waiting room chair and watching him pop another chip into his mouth, I suddenly realize that I am waiting for *something*.

He has been here supporting me, taking shifts guarding Owen, and yet I feel like I am stuck in limbo.

Our relationship, if I can even call it that, is completely undefined.

I don't know where I stand and I don't know what we're doing.

What is this exactly?

It wasn't that long ago when he was just a mysterious stranger who made me an unbelievable offer that I was just crazy enough to accept and give up my job for.

But what about now?

I'm not just his employee anymore.

We're more than that.

We have this explosive chemistry and impossible need to be together physically, but...is that enough?

Is that it?

I know that it's not *it* for me.

I want more.

I feel like he wants more, too. Why else would he spend his days here with me?

People are out to get him and it's probably best for him to not be in Boston anymore, and yet here he is.

He's staying by my side.

That means something. No, it means everything. And yet, there are still lingering questions that need answers.

"So...are there any new jobs on the horizon?" I ask, spinning my ring around my index finger.

"No, not really," he says, taking a sip of his coffee.

"Is that because there are no jobs or because you are giving me a break?" I press.

"There are no jobs," he says earnestly.

It's meant to feel like he's telling me the truth but it doesn't feel like it *is* the truth.

When I push him more, he stands his ground.

This isn't going anywhere. I don't even know why I brought it up since it's not really anything that I'm particularly interested in discussing.

What I really want to know is where we are as a couple.

What are we doing?

I want to define who we are.

I want to know if I'm his girlfriend and he's my boyfriend.

We've talked about being exclusive but that doesn't seem enough right now.

I want him to tell me that he's in love with me.

I wish I could just open my mouth and say that to him.

But when I do, that's not what comes out at all.

"Do you have money?" I ask.

The bluntness of the question takes both of us by surprise.

He gives me a long, careful stare. His eyes narrow and widen before he looks away and brings his cup to his lips.

"What are you talking about?" he asks, mumbling through a sip.

I take a deep breath.

"Is that the only reason you're with me?" he asks after a long pause.

"No, of course not," I say a little bit too quickly.

When I force myself to look at him, I know immediately that I haven't convinced him.

"Sort of feels like it."

"No, not at all." I put my hand on his.

Why are we talking about this?

Why did I blurt that out?

The words just got away from me and now I'm stuck having another conversation that I really don't want to have.

When I look up at him and lose myself in the speck of gold in his eyes, I wait for him to tell me he loves me.

It's stupid and irrational but I still wait.

"Olive, what's going on?" Nicholas says, pulling his hand away from me.

He puts his cup on the table and waits.

I insist that nothing is going on over and over again, but it doesn't change anything.

It doesn't make this wedge that I have created between us get any smaller.

"I just want you to know that it's okay if you... don't," I finally say.

It's not true.

Nothing about that would be okay and yet my lips seem to have a mind of their own.

I quit my job.

I took a chance at starting another life even though it was a mistake like all of those other mistakes that I have made.

When he paid off my debts, I felt indebted to him.

And the money made it all that much easier to make bad decisions.

But there is no such thing as easy money.

It all comes with baggage and consequences.

How many times do I have to learn this lesson?

The conversation shifts to Sydney and then James and then her mother.

I tell Nicholas about how certain James was that her mother would love him and how certain Sydney was that she wouldn't.

I side with Sydney but Nicholas sides with James, saying that there aren't many mothers who wouldn't be impressed with him as a potential son-in-law.

The ebb and flow of a conversation are similar to a tide. It comes and goes in regular intervals and then there are those mysterious shifts that come from somewhere deep below and take you completely by surprise.

"Please don't lie to me, Nicholas," I say quietly. "I can take anything but that."

I look straight at him and ask him again if he's telling me the truth. He pauses for a moment and promises that he is.

7

NICHOLAS
WHEN LIES START TO PILE UP...

I am lying.

Olive gave me so many outs. There were so many opportunities to tell her the truth and yet I can't bring myself to say it.

The thing about truth is that sometimes it's the easiest thing to say in the world.

And other times, it's like admitting defeat and burying yourself underneath the rubble that is your life.

Lies have a way of piling up on top of each other.

You say one lie to cover up another and then another and then another.

I know this.

Everyone over the age of ten knows this and yet we all still do it.

Why?

In the moment, it is too hard to tell the truth.

I want to believe that I'm lying to her to protect her. I want to believe that there is some greater good in all of this.

But the truth is I was too much of a coward to come out and say it. That kind of blow my ego couldn't handle.

I don't know what I'm doing.

This whole thing started as a way to protect her.

I made a promise to my dead little sister and I wanted that to be the one promise that I kept in my life.

But then things got complicated.

The money was an exaggeration.

What I had, what was mine, it was all for show.

Well, no, that's not quite true. There was a time when I had it all. And then I lost it all.

That sort of thing happens when the money doesn't really belong to you.

It comes into your life like an avalanche.

It's all at once and it overwhelms you with possibilities.

But then it tends to leave just as fast.

You make plans, you try to save, you try to start a new life but you can't.

I've seen it happen to people on the streets and now it has happened to me.

After it's gone, the only thing it leaves is a trail of *what-ifs*.

I don't know how Olive would react if I were to come right out and tell her all of this.

Maybe she would hate me or dump me or maybe she would think it's the best thing that could have happened because it takes her off the hook for the rest of the year.

She doesn't know this but I see the way that she's looking at me. I see her second-guessing me. I see the regret in her eyes.

Before Owen got hurt, I thought that maybe there was a chance that we could start a life somewhere.

A real life.

We were so close to that. The job was done. I had some money. I could tell her the truth about...everything.

She'd be angry but maybe she could find it in her heart to forgive me.

But now? Now, suddenly, everything is different. The people who shot Owen didn't finish the job and they are probably just waiting for the chance to complete it.

She knows that Owen isn't her real brother and that she has a biological mother somewhere out there. And that's the kind of loose strings that tend to tear apart undefined plans.

Even though she hasn't said anything out loud, I know that the only thing that she is probably thinking about now is this other family.

Who are they? Why did her real mother give her up? Where does she live? And how long would it take for her to get to her?

"So, what do you think about Owen?" I finally ask her.

This question has been on the tip of my tongue ever since she came to the hospital last night. "What do you think about him not being your real brother?"

"I don't know what to think," she says, staring into space.

I try to imagine how I would feel if Ashley wasn't my real sister.

But I don't feel any different. The biology doesn't seem to matter. She's my sister because I have always believed her to be.

Yet, when I look over at Olive, I realize that that's not exactly how she feels.

"He's still going to be my brother," she says, definitively with a stern nod.

It's as if she is trying to convince herself of something, something she doesn't want to believe.

"Yeah, he will," I lie.

Another lie to cover up what I really think. And what is that exactly? I wonder. What is this hesitation in her demeanor?

"Apparently, Owen knew that he wasn't my real brother," Olive says quietly.

I stare at her as the pieces of the puzzle start to fall into place.

Of course. That's why he has been acting this way.

I thought he was just a concerned brother.

I thought that he was just someone who was a little bit too involved in her life, but then again, he did get paroled to her home and she was his only friend in the outside world.

I tried to make myself believe that this was the end of the story. But now, it all makes sense.

"He's in love with you," I say under my breath with the realization dawning on me only when the words escape my lips.

"No...wait, what?" she asks, sitting up in her chair and looking at me surprised.

"That's why he has been acting so... possessive. It wasn't just brotherly love. He loves you in a different way, Olive."

"No, c'mon, that's...gross," she says.

Her words are cautious.

It's as if I am not telling her something that she doesn't already know.

Looking her up and down, I realize that this is not news to her. She clumsily tries to cover it up with a head shake and a look of shock on her face but I can feel it in my gut that I'm right.

I didn't realize how right I was until this very moment.

8

NICHOLAS

WHEN I SEARCH FOR THE TRUTH...

I know that she's lying about Owen and I know that I'm lying about my bank account. Yet, both lies seem somehow inevitable.

Is that what we are becoming now?

Two people who lie to each other about who they really are?

If so, then why even bother going on?

Why even bother pursuing this any longer?

This wasn't the first time that this thought crossed my mind.

Things would definitely be a lot easier if Olive wasn't in my life.

I would be a one-man show, responsible for no one.

I would be able to work for Hawk and keep the FBI at bay.

I wouldn't have anyone to worry about. I wouldn't have an obligation.

But I know that I can' take myself *there*. Olive isn't a loose string. I can force myself to cut it off but what would I have? Being with her makes me feel alive and I haven't felt that for a very long time.

The wind picks up and I put up my collar to keep it at bay.

Why can't we have this meeting at a coffee shop or a restaurant, I have no idea. But it's his call.

He shows up ten minutes later, half an hour late. I wait for him to apologize but he doesn't offer even a cursory *I'm sorry*.

I don't press it because I want to know what he has found.

"Don't you just love this weather?" Kip Flunderson, the investigator says with a wide, beaming smile across his face.

He is in his sixties with broad shoulders and a casual attitude.

A little too casual if you ask me.

"I'm not a fan of the cold," I say with a shrug.

He laughs and waves me off as if I'm a fly.

I cross my arms across my chest and shift my weight to the back foot. I kick myself for not stopping for a cup of coffee before coming here.

I had plenty of time since he was half an hour late and didn't bother to leave me a text.

"Are you okay?" Kip asks.

"Yes," I lie. "No."

"Which is it?"

"I wish you had told me you were going to be late," I blurt out, annoyed.

"I don't text, kid," Kip says with that same annoying grin.

"You could have called," I point out. "Anything would've been good."

Kip opens his jacket and pulls out a manila folder. "How about this?" he asks, holding it out to me.

"What's this?" I ask, taking it.

"It's everything about Olive Kernes' mother. Her name. Where she lives. Who she is. Who her family is."

I open the file and start to peruse the paperwork. The sheer quantity of it takes me by surprise.

"Wow," I finally say, a little out of breath.

"How did you find this?"

"That's for me to know and for you to pay me for," Kip says with his eyes twinkling under the streetlights.

Suddenly, waiting all of this time on the bench overlooking the pond sounds like a small price to pay, along with the actual price of ten thousand dollars.

"You know, I didn't think there would be so much information about that adoption," I say.

"Okay, now, Nicholas, tell the truth," Kip says. "You didn't think that an old man like me who refuses to communicate via texts would be able to find much of anything."

"Yeah." I give him a nod, admitting defeat. "You got me there."

I hand him the envelope with the ten grand in crisp one hundred dollar bills.

He looks at it, peruses the hundreds but doesn't count it. Instead, he looks at the size of the stack and then puts it in his pocket.

"So, are you sure that this is her?" I ask, nodding at the folder in my hand.

"Absolutely."

"But...how can you be so sure?"

"Take it with you. Read through it. If you aren't satisfied, reach out to me and we'll talk. I'll give you a full refund if you find any discrepancies in that file."

"Really?" I'm taken aback a little bit. "Wow."

"I stand behind my work 100%."

"Yes, I guess so," I say, holding out my hand to him.

His grip is strong and forceful but not like he's trying hard to impress me.

I wait for him to disappear down the street before I sit back down on the bench and open the folder.

———

I CAN BARELY FEEL my hands by the time I get to the last page of the folder but I know one thing for sure. This is her mother and everything in this packet has to be true.

It isn't organized very well or even in any logical manner, but somewhere in the middle of the pile are the results of the DNA test.

Apparently, during these last few weeks, Kip had the time to stalk both Olive and her mother and get samples of their DNA.

I don't know exactly how he did it but I imagine discarded coffee cups were involved in some way.

In any case, they are a match.

There is a 99.999% certainty that this is her mother.

There is only one thing left to do now; tell Olive.

I put the file safely into my jacket and zip it over it.

It makes a crinkling sound as I walk but I can barely hear it over the pounding of my heartbeat in my head.

This folder feels like it's going to fix everything. It's going to make every weirdness between us disappear and make her mine again.

It's going to be just like it was in the beginning.

It's going to ignite that spark that pulled us close together and made it impossible for us to stay away from each other.

When I get to the hospital, I look for her in the waiting room, but she's nowhere to be found.

She's probably in the bathroom, I say to myself and take a seat.

The hospital feels warm and cozy and I don't unzip my jacket to cocoon some of that feeling.

"Oh, hey, Marlene!" I yell out to one of the nurses walking briskly past me. "Have you seen Olive recently?"

"You haven't heard?" she asks with a huge toothy grin. "He's awake."

9

NICHOLAS
WHEN HE WAKES UP…

I hear the hesitation in my knock when my knuckles collide with the wood.

An eternity passes before anyone answers.

I knock again.

Louder this time.

Again, no one answers.

When no one responds, I turn the knob.

I can hear her voice inside.

When I crack the door, Olive's excitement and exuberance spills out into the hallway.

"Hey...Owen...you're awake," I say, walking in.

He is pale and his lips are chapped but there is an inkling of a smile on his face.

Olive waves me over to the bed.

She is talking nonstop and neither Owen nor I try to get a word in edgewise.

Her fingers are intertwined with his and there are dried tears on her cheeks.

"How are you?" I ask when she stops for some air.

I half expect him to get angry at me, but instead he just nods and whispers, "I'm good."

His voice is raspy, barely audible but I get the sense that he's happy to see me.

Or at the very least, not upset that I'm here.

Olive tells him how we have all been waiting around the clock for him to wake up outside and how happy we all are that he's finally back.

"You both, and Mom?" Owen asks slowly, clearing his throat in the middle.

His question is like a punch to the gut to Olive.

She recoils a little bit but quickly gathers her footing and lies.

"Yes, us and Mom," she lies, squeezing his hand.

When our eyes meet, hers dart away.

We both know that their mother hasn't been around much.

If she had come here three times over the last month and stayed for more than two hours that would be stretching the truth.

But Owen doesn't need to know that.

No one wants to hear that about someone who is supposed to love them unconditionally.

"Actually, not just us," Olive adds. "Sydney and James as well."

"Your roommate?" Owen asks.

Olive nods, rubbing her hand on his.

"Yeah, my roommate and her boyfriend James. He's actually a really awesome guy. A friend of Nicholas' from Hawaii. Isn't that right?"

Owen gives me a nod.

"Yep, he's great," I agree.

"Why...were...they...here?"

"To wait for you, silly," Olive says. "To help me wait for you to wake up."

Owen looks up at the ceiling.

I watch him examine each tile individually before moving on to the next and then make his way toward the window.

"You...thought that...someone would come here and...kill me, huh?" Owen says after a long pause.

"No, of course not," Olive lies.

She squeezes his hand and makes him look at her.

"I just wanted someone to be here the moment you woke up," she says. We all know that's not true.

When he opens his mouth to say something else, she shuts him down.

"Let's not talk about that now. We can get to all of that later."

————

IT's hard to explain what it feels like to be in this room with Olive and Owen.

I am happy that he is better.

I am happy that the doctor said that he will make a full recovery and yet something feels off.

Suddenly, I am an outsider.

The bond that Olive and Owen have is difficult to describe.

On one hand, they are close like a brother and a sister but, on the other, there is more depth there as well, particularly on his part.

When they started writing those letters to each other, Owen knew the truth about their biology. Now, the pieces are starting to fall into place.

The fact that they are not related to each other explains so much about how he was acting before his coma. He wasn't just the big brother looking out for his little sister.

He had been harboring these feelings for her and now that everything is out in the open, their bond seems impossible to penetrate.

I hate it when I let myself go to these dark places.

I try to act like an optimist most of the time but if I were telling the truth, I am not one.

I try to put on a good show but it's hard.

I have been through so much and have experienced so much darkness that I find myself holding my breath for the next bad thing to happen.

Of course, just because Owen feels like he feels about Olive that doesn't mean that she feels the same way about him.

She has always loved him like a brother and just because she found out that they are not biologically related that doesn't mean that she will magically fall in love with him.

That doesn't mean that her feelings will suddenly turn sexual.

It doesn't mean that I have anything to worry about. Right?

10

NICHOLAS

WHEN WE RECONNECT…

*I*t has been two days since Owen woke up. It has been two days since I've seen Olive.

I haven't been back to the hospital since, and Olive hasn't left his side.

Tonight, she's finally coming back.

I'm making dinner. Sydney and James are staying at a hotel for the night.

We have the place to ourselves.

Tonight will be the night when our relationship will hit the reset button.

I hear her key in the door right at seven, just as I put the salmon and the asparagus on her stove.

"Wow, this smells delicious," she says, giving me a big kiss. "Do you mind if I jump into the shower? I've been wearing these clothes for days."

"No problem," I say. "This isn't going to be ready for a bit. You want me to join you?"

She laughs, tossing her hair back. "No, I'm good. Besides, our dinner will probably burn then."

I take a deep breath and let it out slowly. That wasn't meant to be an insult so why did it sound so much like one?

No, take it easy. Don't read into everything.

She is going through a lot, you have to give her some space, I say to myself. All she needs is some time.

The food is almost ready when she emerges from her room and sits down at the table.

Dressed in a clean, loose-fitting t-shirt and yoga pants, she pours herself a glass of wine.

Her hair is wet, dripping down her shirt, and her face is clean without a smudge of makeup.

I lose my ability to speak for a moment as I stare at the most beautiful woman in the world.

Olive rips into a hunk of unsliced bread that I set out on the table, washing it down with two big gulps of wine.

"Oh my god, this tastes so good," she says, pushing her hair out of her face. "It feels so good to be home."

"It's nice to have you," I say.

There are so many things to talk about: the file that I got on her real mother, the fact that I don't want to keep squatting in this small apartment with two other roommates, the possibility that her brother might be in love with her.

And yet, I don't dare to bring up any of these issues.

This moment is just for us.

We need to reconnect.

We need to be with each other again.

That's the only thing that's going to stop this wedge that has formed between us from growing wider and deeper.

"Wait," she says, pulling the glass away from her lips. "Before we dive into this wonderful dinner that you made, I want to make a toast."

"Okay." I put my fork down.

"I want to thank you for being the most wonderful boyfriend ever," she says, raising her arm higher. "I really don't know what I would've done without you. You waited in the hospital for him so that I could get some rest, all of those nights and days and hours."

"It was nothing," I interrupt even though it means a lot that she is so appreciative of it.

"No, it wasn't nothing. You are not Owen's biggest fan but you did it for me and I want you to know that I appreciate it. I really do."

"Well...thank you," I say. "I was happy to do it."

She looks into my eyes and I look into hers.

We lose each other there for a long while.

At first, it feels comfortable, but then somehow it doesn't. It dawns on me that she's waiting for something.

She's waiting for me to say, "I love you."

I open my lips and clear my throat.

The words are on the tip of my tongue. It's so simple.

People say it all the time.

And yet...for some reason, I can't.

What's worse is that the feeling overwhelms me.

I know that I love her and there will never be anyone I will care about more.

And yet, I can't bring myself to say those three simple words.

What am I afraid of? They will never do me any harm. If anything they will set me free.

"I…"

I see her holding her breath.

She's waiting for me to say it. Three simple words.

Just finish the sentence.

You can do it, I say to myself.

"Yes?" Olive asks hopefully.

"I just wanted to say…do you want more pepper on that?"

The disappointment that floods her face is difficult to describe but it hurts me to my core.

My whole body shudders.

But the moment passes.

If I couldn't say it earlier, now the statement becomes an impossibility.

For the rest of dinner we talk about anything and everything. Olive tells me about how Owen is doing in recovery and how excited she is to see him get stronger with each day.

I smile and act excited all the while hoping that she doesn't see my disappointment.

I'm not disappointed with Owen. I am happy for him and I am glad that Olive is no longer worried about him.

What I am is disappointed in myself. Even though we are having this nice dinner and everything is pleasant, there still seems to be a river rushing between us.

There are all of these things left unsaid.

All of these things that we haven't talked about.

And the longer we don't talk about the real things, the bigger the river gets.

When Olive helps me clear the table, I lean over and kiss her. She's surprised at first and pulls away, but only briefly.

My fingers run down her body as she buries her hands in my hair. Pushing her against the wall, I press myself against hers.

Our mouths find each other and our tongues intertwine.

We don't bother to take off most of our clothes.

Our movements are hurried and out of control.

We need to be together as quickly as possible. Unlike before when we took our time and paced ourselves, this time we don't.

Her legs open for me as she presses her face toward the wall and props up her butt.

I cup it only for a second before sliding inside.

Her moans become my moans.

We move in unison, riding the same wave.

I hear her getting close and try to last a little bit longer.

When she yells my name, I finally let myself go.

11

OLIVE
WHEN HE COMES HOME...

I don't know what's different between Nicholas and I but something is very...uneven.

I care about him. A lot.

I even love him, but ever since Owen woke up, everything feels forced.

No, if I were telling the truth, things have felt off since Owen was in the hospital.

It's almost as if there's some sort of disconnect between us.

I thought that maybe tonight it would finally go away. He made me this wonderful dinner.

I was so happy to be home and all I wanted to do was celebrate.

We had this moment when I thought that Nicholas would take me into his arms and finally tell me that he's in love with me.

That would make things not feel so off.

But instead, he just...let it go.

Maybe I should've said it first.

Maybe I shouldn't have been such a wimp. But I got scared.

What if he doesn't love me? What if me saying it would just make things even worse between us?

And then when he kissed me, I kissed him back.

I wanted him.

I wanted to feel his body next to mine, on top of mine, inside of mine.

But having sex just cast a spotlight on everything that is wrong between us.

Whatever is going on, I have to put it out of my mind.

At least for now.

Owen is coming home this afternoon. The living situation here is getting a bit cramped so Nicholas is getting a hotel.

Owen offered to stay at our mom's but that is out of the question.

She didn't bother to come see him much in the hospital and knowing her, he would be there taking care of her more than she would him.

No, staying here is the best choice.

I will just sleep on the couch and he can have my room. Luckily, Sydney and James are okay with it for now.

————

OWEN COMES HOME LATER that afternoon. He manages to walk inside without using the wheelchair that the hospital insisted that he take, but he does collapse onto the couch soon after.

The doctors warned him that he will feel incredibly tired for days or even weeks to come and that we should expect that.

I take a seat next to him and put his hand into mine.

I'm glad that he's here. Somewhere safe.

Later that evening, that general feeling that everything is safe wears off.

We talk about everything and nothing at all and have a nice dinner, but dark thoughts start to haunt me.

"Are you okay?" Owen asks, spreading out on the couch.

"Yes, I'm fine," I lie.

When he asks me again, I lie again. But he doesn't let it go.

"People are still after you," I finally cave.

He shrugs.

"They tried to kill you once, they're probably going to do it again."

He shrugs again.

"Don't you care?"

"Yes, I do, but I'm not sure what exactly I can do about it."

I admit that I don't either.

We sit for a while, nursing our drinks and thinking all of the bad things that we are too afraid to say out loud.

There's something else, of course. His physical safety is not the only thing on my mind.

"You're not my brother," I say.

The words slip out of me before I can catch myself. Owen stares at me for a long time before saying anything.

"No, I'm not."

I wait for him to ask me how I know, but he doesn't.

He just repeats that he's not my brother, as a matter of fact. As if it's something that we have both known for a very long time.

"Why didn't you tell me?" I ask.

"I couldn't find a good time."

"How about when you wrote me all of those letters? During all of those years?"

He takes a deep breath and then lets it out slowly as if he were exhaling a cigarette.

He raises his shoulders and lets them down gently.

"Tell me the truth," I demand. "Don't lie to me."

There's another deep breath.

Then, there's another deep exhalation.

I wait.

"I didn't want anything between us to change. You were there for me and you were the only family I had. I didn't want our DNA to change that."

"So, you were just...using me?" I ask.

"No, not at all. I love you, Olive."

The words send shivers down my spine.

I stare into his eyes. His irises are dark and full of depth.

He blinks and I see the glimpse of the sorrow.

I don't know what he means by that.

Does he love me like a sister? Or does he love me as more than that? He doesn't elaborate and I don't dare to ask.

"I wrote you all of those letters because you were the only person there for me, Olive. I wanted to know about your life. I wanted to tell you about mine," he says.

The words are difficult for him to say and his voice cracks throughout.

"You are my family no matter what," he adds. "I don't care that we're not actually biologically related."

I nod. Tears start to well up in the bottom of my eyes.

"I don't care either," I say with a sob. "I love you, too, Owen."

I have waited for so long for him to get out and then for so long for him to wake up.

It feels like a big portion of my life has revolved around waiting. And now that he's here...I'm afraid that I might lose him forever.

We hold each other for a while without saying a word. It feels good to be held by him. There isn't anything romantic or sexual about it. He's just my brother and nothing is going to change that.

The only reason we pull away is when we hear Sydney's key rattling in the door.

James is with her and they arrive with food and smiles on their faces to welcome Owen home.

While she arranges the takeout containers on the coffee table for everyone to eat family style, I sense the tension between them.

"What's wrong?" I ask Sydney in a quiet whisper while we pull plates from the cupboard. "Are you okay?"

"We had a fight." She rolls her eyes.

"Wow, is that like the first one for you two?" I joke.

"Hardly." She shakes her head.

I purse my lips, genuinely surprised. "Really?" I ask.

She shakes her head dismissively.

"Why didn't you tell me?"

"You're going through a lot of shit, I'm not going to bother you about every stupid little tiff."

"No, no! Don't do that. Don't say that. You're my best friend. I need to know what's going on with you."

"Well, you haven't been around much, Olive."

She walks over to the coffee table and sets down the cutlery.

I feel like a fool. No, more like a stupid, self-absorbed little girl.

I've been going through a lot but she's right. I have neglected her.

When was the last time we actually spoke to each other? I can't even remember.

Is her mother still in town? I don't know.

Sydney and I both make a considerable effort to not make dinner awkward. Owen and James talk about sports, not noticing a thing. She's being friendly to both James and me for Owen's benefit. Friendly but not fake-friendly.

After loading the dishwasher, James goes for a run and I help Owen get into bed.

I'm giving him my room so that he can get plenty of rest on the bed while I take the couch.

After I tuck him in and turn off the light, I knock on Sydney's door.

12

OLIVE

WHEN WE TALK...

*S*ydney doesn't answer the door so I force myself in. I sit down on the bed next to her. She turns away from me and crosses her arms.

"Can we talk?" I ask.

She pulls out a jar from her nightstand and points the round mirror toward her face. Unscrewing the top, she grabs a generous amount of mud and starts spreading it on her face.

"You want some?" she asks after a moment.

"Sure." I nod.

I appreciate the gesture and I'm not about to turn away the olive branch just because I'm still wearing makeup.

"I'm sorry I've been so...absent recently. You're really important to me and I just want you to know that."

"It's fine, really. I was just really pissed off at James and I shouldn't have taken it out on you."

"What's going on?" I ask, just realizing that I had completely forgotten to ask how the brunch at the Ritz went with her mom and James.

"I really thought that she wasn't going to like him. I mean, she hasn't liked anyone, right? Well, she likes him. A little bit too much!"

"Really?"

"It's nauseating," Sydney says, turning her face toward me. "I mean, she's like obsessed with him. She keeps asking me where we stand and when we are taking things to the next level. She thinks he's a total catch."

"Well, he is."

"Yes, but so what? I'm a catch, too."

"I don't think anyone is denying that."

Sydney shakes her head and looks down at the floor.

"What's wrong?" I ask, putting my arm around her shoulder.

Thick round tears start to roll down her cheeks.

"It's her," she whispers when she finally manages to gather her thoughts. "It's always her."

I let out a deep sigh.

Like any mother, Hilary possesses the immeasurable power to make her daughter feel like she's worthless.

Not all mothers choose to wield this power, and some do despite their best efforts.

But Hilary uses it expertly.

"I'm never good enough, Olive. Nothing I ever do is good enough."

"You're a wonderful person," I whisper into her ear, trying to make up for all of her mother's shortcomings. "It doesn't matter what she says. Or thinks."

"I know that." Sydney nods. "Of course, I know that. But it doesn't change the fact that she's my mother and...I want her to be proud of me."

"I'm sure she is," I lie.

In reality, I have no idea and I have plenty of doubts.

If Sydney had a normal mother, her prestigious college degree and her well-paying job would be a source of pride. But in Hilary's ledger, she's barely meeting minimal expectations.

And when it comes to looks, Sydney falls far below those expectations.

"What did she say to you this time?"

Sydney wipes her eyes and shakes her head.

She opens her mouth, but the words come out in a jumble and she starts to cry again.

On the surface, our mothers couldn't be any more different but they are identical in how they make us feel.

No matter what we do, we are never good enough.

In her case, Sydney will never be pretty enough or thin enough or smart enough to please her mother.

In my case, I will never be good enough because I'm not my oldest brother.

Hilary's cruelty is a bit different from my mother's because with her everything simmers in the shadows.

She will never come right out and tell Sydney that she thinks she's fat, but she will make comments and insinuations that make that perfectly clear.

The few times that Sydney called her on it, Hilary denied it wholeheartedly, promising that she was just joking and asking Sydney why she has such a terrible sense of humor (an insult wrapped in an insult).

"So, she really likes James?" I ask, trying to get her to open up to me.

"Yes. A lot."

I smile.

"I know." Sydney nods. "I was just as shocked as you were. I mean, James wasn't, but what does he know about Hilary, right?"

"So, what happened?" I ask.

"Brunch at the Ritz went without a hitch. He buttered her up and she ate it all up. Halfway through, I started thinking that she was just putting on an act and that I'll hear all about how awful he is afterward but I didn't. She actually liked him."

"That's great," I say.

She pulls away from me.

The expression on her face tells me that maybe it's not as great as I thought.

"What's wrong with that?" I ask.

"Now, she's asking me about where everything is going. All the time. She wants us to move in together. She is hinting at us getting married. And if it doesn't happen, I know that she is going to put all the blame on me."

"Get married?" I ask. "But you just met."

Sydney shrugs and rolls her eyes.

"But you don't even want to get married, right?"

"No, not really. I mean, I want to be with James. I love him. But the fact that my mother actually likes him, and not just that, likes him a lot...it's really making me question what I think about him."

"Okay, don't do that," I say quickly. "Don't let her muddle you. You love him. You want to be with him. It's a good thing that she likes him and it doesn't mean that you have to re-think anything about him or your relationship."

"Don't you see how sick that is?" Sydney asks. "How fucked up? Everyone thinks we have this great mother-daughter relationship, when in reality, it's nothing but a hall of mirrors."

I want to bring up that my own relationship with my mother is just as messed up but I don't want to make this a competition for who has the worst mother.

She is going through something serious right now and I want to acknowledge that.

I want to be here for her in every way that I haven't been this whole time.

I don't know what else to say so I just wrap my arms around her and hold her for a while.

"Think of it this way," I mutter after a few minutes. "No matter how much your mom approves of James now, you know that she would never approve of your open relationship and your sex life."

Sydney starts to laugh.

Thank God.

That's exactly the effect that I was going for.

"It almost makes me want to tell her," she says.

"Don't. At least not now. You need to save that for a rainy day."

"If even then," she says after a moment when her smile goes away. "She'd hate him and she'd never let it go. We'd never get over it."

I give her a nod.

She's absolutely right.

If Hilary were to ever find out about their less than vanilla bedroom antics, she would do everything in her power to drive a wedge in between them.

No, it's better to just imagine the look on her face if she were ever to find out rather than actually dealing with the repercussions.

"I'm sorry, I got so upset with you earlier," Sydney says, turning her body toward me and sitting up higher on the bed. "She was just making all of these jokes about my body and how fat I was without really coming out and saying I was fat and it just made me feel...terrible."

"Please, you don't have to apologize. I haven't been a good friend to you for a while. I'm so sorry that your mom is like that. You're beautiful, you know that, right?"

She nods, but I am not convinced.

I put my finger under her chin and force her eyes to meet mine.

"You are amazing and beautiful and gorgeous. I don't know why your mother says those things but you can't let yourself believe them."

A tear rolls off her cheek, but this one is a happy tear.

She wraps her arms around me and holds on tightly.

13

NICHOLAS
WHEN WE MEET AGAIN...

I arrive at the bar early to get a drink before our meeting. These meetings never go well since I hate the sight and smell of him and have no idea how to extricate him from my life.

Well, that's not exactly true, I say to myself taking a sip of the whiskey from the top shelf.

It's dark and rich and makes me feel momentarily better about my situation.

There is one thing that I can do that would solve all of my problems.

I can disappear.

I did a bit of that in Hawaii but it wasn't a valiant effort. I used my name.

I relied on old contacts to make new friends.

I relied on my reputation to do what I thought I needed.

But what if I didn't?

What if I actually vanished?

Completely?

New name.

New identity.

New way of life.

People do it all the time. I have skills that will keep me afloat while I try to figure it all out and start a new life.

You wouldn't believe how many people are officially living under new identities through the Witness Protection Program and how many thousands more are doing it unofficially.

I could be that statistic.

Starting a new life in a new place would solve all of my problems.

If I do it right, not the FBI, nor the police, nor anyone else in the government would be able to find me.

First of all, I haven't murdered anyone and so far, the case they were trying to make against me for supposedly killing my old partner isn't really a case at all.

Thus, they'd have a harder time getting my story onto America's Most Wanted and other television programs that enlist the public's help in looking for fugitives.

If I vanish and start a new life, I wouldn't have to work for the FBI gathering evidence on Olive's brother and I wouldn't have to worry about the debt that the mob thinks I owe them.

No one would be able to find me.

There is only one hiccup in this proposition. Olive Kernes.

I haven't told her I love her, but I do. More than anything. I want her to come with me, but I am afraid to ask.

I am afraid of her saying *no*.

I can't tell her about my relationship with the FBI and I certainly can't tell her about them wanting me to gather information about Owen.

So far, Owen can do no wrong in her eyes.

So far, Owen is a god and until that changes, she will take his side if she were to find out the truth about me.

The other option is to lie to her. I can tell her that I need to disappear because of the people who are after me.

They are threatening my life and the only way out is to not be here anymore and to not be Nicholas Crawford.

She cares about me and she would worry, but is that enough?

Her brother is in the exact same situation and he just got out of a coma that came as a result of someone actually trying to kill him.

She wouldn't disappear on him.

She wouldn't start a new life with me and leave him behind.

But what if there were another option?

That thought had never crossed my mind before, and even now, nursing the second glass of whiskey, it sends shivers through me.

I don't like Owen and he hates me.

We don't have a good history but that doesn't mean that we can't find common ground in order to preserve both of our hides.

How does that saying go again?

The enemy of my enemy is my friend? Maybe that's it. Maybe that's the solution to all of our problems?

Taking another sip, I run my fingers over the grain of the bartop.

There are thick impressions in it from years of wear, giving it character and the well-worn look of a place where many people sat and buried their problems at the bottom of a bottle.

More thoughts flood into my mind.

The results of the DNA test that prove the real identity of Olive's mother are still sitting in a folder in my car's glove compartment.

I was going to hand her all of the information about who she really is and wait for her to throw her arms around my neck and kiss me like she never kissed me before. But I never found the right time.

Perhaps, there is no right time.

"Sorry I'm late," Art says, taking the seat next to me.

This is the first time he has ever apologized for this and I wouldn't be surprised if this is the first time he has ever said he was sorry about anything.

"No worries," I say. "Had a good drink to keep me company."

"I'll have what he's having," Art tells the bartender. "So, how are you doing, Nicholas?"

Now, I know that something is up. The Art Hedison I know loves nothing more than to put me in my place by calling me Nicky.

"I'm good," I say without missing a beat.

"Haven't seen you in a while," Art says.

I shrug. "That's more up to you than to me. And Owen has been rather indisposed."

"How's he feeling?"

"Good. They discharged him. No memory loss. I'm not sure he's fully physically back but you know..." I say.

I'm not revealing anything he doesn't already know.

I haven't seen him at the hospital, of course, but I'm sure that his office has had a watchful eye over the place, if not direct contact with his doctors and nurses.

"He still hates me, in case you're wondering," I add. "So I haven't found out anything more than what I told you before."

Art takes a few satisfying gulps of his whiskey and asks the bartender for a refill.

Suddenly, it dawns on me that this meeting might not be about Owen at all.

14

NICHOLAS

WHEN HE TELLS ME WHAT HE REALLY WANTS…

I wait silently for Art to say something but he doesn't. He just swishes the whiskey in his glass round and round.

I'm tempted to pester him but I decide to bide my time.

If he wants something from me and needs to build up the courage to ask, then I will just wait.

"Let's go talk somewhere else," he says.

He pays both of our tabs and I follow him outside.

I assume we're going to go back to the alley where we usually do our business.

It's long and narrow with no windows pointed at it from the nearby windows making it the perfect place to talk about private things.

But he surprises me once again.

He leads me to the brightly lit diner across the street.

It's pretty empty and he takes a seat in a booth at the far end, as far away from prying ears as possible.

When the waitress comes with our coffees, I order the number three breakfast with scrambled eggs, sourdough toast, and an avocado on the side.

Art asks for a stack of pancakes with eggs.

While we wait, I'm again tempted to ask him what he wants but I again force myself to wait.

I don't want to make this easy for him.

If he wants to ask me a favor, which at this point I'm pretty sure he does, he'll have to actually ask.

"I need your help," Art says, looking me straight in the eye.

Unlike in the bar where we were sitting shoulder to shoulder, here in this booth, directly across from each other, there is nowhere to hide so he doesn't bother.

"What kind of help?" I ask.

Art looks around and lowers his voice. "Let me see your phone," he finally says.

I pull it out of my pocket and lay it on the table.

"You're not recording this, right?" he asks.

Wow, this must be serious if he's worried that I'm recording *him*.

In my line of work, the last thing you want is to carry around proof that you are talking to the authorities.

"No, of course not," I say.

He asks to see my phone again and doesn't say another word until he searches through it to make sure there isn't any recording going on in any hidden folders.

When he is satisfied, he hands it back to me and picks up his coffee cup.

"Are you going to tell me what's going on?" I ask just as the waitress comes back with our enormous plates of food.

He waits for her to walk away before looking back at me.

"I owe somebody a debt," Art finally says. "It's pretty big."

"How big?"

He doesn't respond.

"What do you want from me?" I ask instead.

"I want you to break into a safe in someone's house and steal a painting," he says quietly, under his breath.

"Why?"

"As a favor."

"What's in it for me?"

"If you do this then you won't have to spy on Owen anymore."

I stare at him for a long time.

This is the only thing I want, the answer to my prayers. But I'm also skeptical.

"I find it hard to believe that your bosses would just let me go...just like that."

He shrugs. "They wouldn't just let you go. Your cover can be compromised, but in a good way."

"And what about the case against me?"

"I can make that go away, too. Evidence can be lost."

"What about Owen? Why would your boss suddenly not care about him anymore?"

Art looks around again, but in a way that would be difficult for anyone else to spot as suspicious.

"His medical file currently says that he has suffered no memory loss, but it doesn't have to continue to say that. Medical records can be fudged. If he is mentally compromised, he is useless to us. The investigation against him will go away."

"All for this?" I ask.

He nods. That's not good enough. I need an explanation.

"Art, you have to tell me more. I need to know what I'm getting myself into," I say, spreading some avocado on my toast and taking a bite.

"I did all the preliminary work. I know this guy and where he keeps the painting. I can give you everything that I have later. All the details. But only after you agree to the deal."

I chew slowly trying to make the feeling that this is all some sort of set-up to put me away for life go away.

"How much money do you owe?"

Art pours a generous amount of maple syrup on his pancakes before answering, "Four-hundred grand."

"Four hundred?" I whisper. He nods.

"You've been a very bad boy, Art."

He shakes his head.

"It wasn't supposed to turn out that way. I only owed one hundred when I lost last week. But then I thought I got a hot streak and I could win it all back. I bet big and then I bet bigger. By the time it was six a.m., I'd lost it all and I was in debt four big ones."

"Fuck me," I whisper under my breath.

"Yep, that's what it felt like at first. And then I realized who I owed the money to."

"Who?" I ask.

Art stares at me as if I've asked the most foolish question in the world.

"Who else?" He laughs.

15

NICHOLAS

WHEN HE TELLS ME WHAT HE REALLY WANTS...

*a*rt doesn't have to give me the name out loud. There's only one person in this town to throw that kind of money on an illegal card game.

"How much time do you have to pay up?" I ask.

"A week."

I laugh, shaking my head. "You're fucked."

"Yes, I know, that's why I'm here talking to *you*."

"Let's say, and that's a very big hypothetical question, but let's say I do get it. What then?

What's this painting going to get you?
Another week? And then what?"

"It's worth seven on the open market and I
have a buyer who will pay me four."

"So, I'm doing this for you for free?" I ask.

"Not exactly. You're buying your freedom. No
more spying on your girlfriend's brother. No
more making a case against bad guys for the
state. You and I are done. I'll make your file
go away and it will never see the light of day."

"You're telling me that a prosecutor isn't
going to find me in a year or two and charge
me with whatever the fuck you all have
on me?"

"Nope," Art says, shaking his head. "I mean,
yes, that's exactly what I'm telling you."

I take another bite and mull everything over.

"What proof would I have that you will keep
your word after I get this painting to you?" I
ask. "That is if I can even get this painting in
the first place."

"You don't."

"What if this is just a trap to get me to do this crime so that you can arrest me?"

"What if it is?" he asks.

"Is it?" I challenge him.

"Absolutely not. Besides, I don't need to trap you. We already have a file on you and that's why we're using you as an informant. This is your opportunity to quit being an informant and get your life back."

I take a sip of my cold, stale coffee and raise the cup in the air for a refill.

We don't say a word to each other while the waitress fills us up.

"I don't know anything about stealing paintings," I say after a while. "I've never taken one before."

"You're in luck then 'cause your girlfriend knows all about it."

This piques my interest.

"Oh, she didn't tell you?" Art asks, leaning close to me. "Well, let me enlighten you."

I try to act like I already know but listen intently.

"When she was in college, she stole a small painting, about an eight by ten. It belonged to the mother of a girl she knew from her British literature class. The owners kept it in a house on Cape Cod and she snuck in and took it from their vault."

I lean back against the back of the booth, trying to fit that into what I already know about Olive and it doesn't fit.

"She didn't replace it with anything," Art says. "Just took it and ran."

"What happened?" I ask.

"On the way out, she got caught by a security guard who she shot in the leg. Luckily, he survived."

I watch his face as he moves his fork around his plate and licks his lips.

His eyes slowly meet mine.

I see a strange look of satisfaction in his eyes.

"I'm not sure if that story is supposed to make me feel better but it doesn't exactly give me a lot of confidence in working with her as a partner."

"She did better the next time," Art says with a smile.

"She did it again?" I ask, raising my eyebrows.

"Two more times. Different people around New England. We're not really sure how she knew all of them. The thing that's particularly curious is that the owners all refused to press charges."

"Huh," I say. "Why is that?"

"The paintings are worth hundreds of thousands of dollars and yet their owners never pressed charges. Why would that be?"

I know the answer as much as he does. I just don't want to say it out loud.

"They were stolen," I finally cave.

"That's right." He smiles his cocky, arrogant, all-knowing smile.

"Who were the artists?" I ask.

"I don't know anything about art but they were all big names. Georgia O'Keeffe, Jenny Saville, Frida Khalo. Sound familiar?"

My mouth nearly drops to the floor. These are some of the best-selling and most respected artists around.

Jenny Saville even set a record for a living female artist when her painting sold for almost twelve and a half million in Sotheby's London.

"So, what happened to these paintings? Sold for a quarter of their value on the black market to some shady collectors who would stick them in a vault and never let them see the light of day?"

"You would think that, wouldn't you?" Art says, laughing. "Nope. They were snuck back into the galleries and museums from which they disappeared. The art directors found them in their offices all the same week."

I stare at him unsure of what to say.

I take another sip of my coffee and Art orders dessert.

The conversation is almost over and yet there is so much left unsaid.

Suddenly, I have more questions than I ever had, yet I don't think the answers are going to be as forthcoming.

"How do you know this?" I finally ask.

"I work for the FBI," he says under his breath. "It's our job to know things, or at least do our best to find out."

"So, you're telling me that Olive, Olive Kernes? My Olive? Is the one who is responsible for stealing those paintings?"

Art nods his head.

"And now you're going to ask her to help you steal another one. For me."

"There's one little snag in your plan, Art," I say. "If she really stole those paintings and just returned them to their rightful owners then she's not going to be too keen in helping me steal a painting for you to pay off your gambling debts."

"Well, it can't all be easy, can it? That's kind of where you come in. It's your job to convince her that it's in her best interest to do this. I mean, it will get the FBI out of Owen's hair, that's for sure. Oh, wait, she doesn't know about that, does she?" He laughs.

I stare at him and shake my head in disbelief.

Even now, even when he is coming to me for assistance, he can't help himself and not be an asshole.

16

NICHOLAS
WHEN SHE COMES OVER...

*a*fter Art leaves, I sit alone in the booth for a long time. The fluorescent lights flicker above my head but I am too preoccupied to let them bother me.

I am having a lot of trouble processing what Art just told me.

Did Olive really steal those paintings? And if so, how?

Did she really just give them back?

No reward, no nothing?

Why?

The answer to the last question escapes me.

If she didn't need the paintings, she could've sold them.

Yes, they would have to be sold on the black market but so what? They were already bought on one.

Once the paintings went missing from the galleries, their owners alerted all of the authorities and no major or reputable art auction house or art dealer would ever deal with them.

But that doesn't mean that Olive couldn't have gotten a nice little nest egg out of it.

My thoughts go in circles until they settle back on Art's proposition.

I help him steal a painting, he sells it, pays his debt, and lets me off the hook.

I don't have to spy and report on Owen anymore.

I don't have to betray Olive anymore or even lie to her.

Running away and hiding out under another identity would be a lot easier if the FBI isn't after me.

If it's just the mob, I can handle it.

As far as I know, they don't yet track credit cards and cell phone towers like the government.

Owen needs to disappear for a bit to get some of the heat off him so maybe an offer for the three of us to go away somewhere would be something that she would consider.

Bringing him along isn't ideal, by any stretch, but it's…something.

It's an option. And Olive and I would still be together.

That can't be bad, right?

———

ART'S PROPOSAL is still heavy on my mind the next day when Olive comes to see me at my hotel room.

We talk about Owen and Sydney and what we should get for dinner.

It feels like there's something else that she wants to bring up and I know that I do. Over some Chinese takeout, I finally ask.

"I have a new job. It's a painting. Are you up for it?"

I look at her trying to gauge her response, but she barely reacts.

"I don't know, Nicholas," she finally says. "I don't know if I'm up for this anymore."

My mouth runs dry.

"What? Why?"

"I'm worried about Owen. We haven't talked about it but those people who tried to kill him, they're still out there. He seems to think that it's all going to be fine, but they tried to kill him once. They'll do it again. And next time, they'll succeed."

"So, what are you planning on doing?"

She puts her hand in mine and looks up at me with her big wide eyes.

"I don't know but I'm not sure I can stay here with him."

"It's not safe. I totally agree."

"You do?" she asks.

"I've been meaning to talk to you about it," I say.

Watching her eyelashes flutter with each breath, I gather my thoughts.

I can sense where she's going with her thinking and, if only I can jump ahead and get there before she does then maybe I have a chance at making this plan come together.

"Owen shouldn't stay in this town. I'm not sure who is after him but we all know that they are very dangerous. He needs to get out of here and he needs money to disappear."

"Disappear?" she whispers.

Her eyes light up for a second but then her shoulders fall.

"No, I don't think-" she starts to say but I interrupt her.

"Hear me out. I need to get out of here, too. But my money is tied up a bit. If you help me get this painting, I can bankroll the whole thing."

One lie rolls into another and another.

I don't have nearly enough for me to start a whole new life, let alone pulling along two other people who would rely on me.

But I need her help.

If she was able to steal those paintings then she is much better at this than I had ever realized.

Hell, she's probably better than I ever was.

"Why did you promise me all of that money if you don't have it?" she asks quietly.

"I do, Olive. I really do. But it's just not all available at once. Besides, you promised to help me in return. This is my next job. Will you do it?"

"How much is the take?"

I let out a big breath.

"It's not that I don't want to work with you anymore, Nicholas. It's just that I can't jeopardize anything happening. I'm lucky to have Owen back in my life, alive and well. I lost him once. I'm not going to do that again."

"That's the whole point, Olive. That's why I need to do this job. It's going to give us enough money to start a whole new life," I say. "That is, unless you want to just start a new life with Owen."

"No, of course not," she says quickly.

"I mean, I know he's not really your brother. You two are close..."

I let my voice trail off and hope she gets the point.

"Don't even go there, Nicholas," she says, making a gross-out face. "He's my brother even if our DNA isn't the same. That's never going to change."

"What about your mother?" I ask.

She sits back on the couch and wraps her arms around her knees. "Now that I'm not so sure about. It's kind of nice having a good reason to get her out of my life. I just wish that I could find out who my real mother is."

I look away.

I'm tempted to pull out that folder and reveal the truth.

Of course, I am. But something stops me.

The folder feels a lot like a Hail Mary and something is telling me to keep it in my back pocket just in case this conversation goes to hell.

"Do this job for me, Olive. This will be it for us," I say, taking her into my arms. "We steal this painting and our original agreement is dissolved. But we can use the money from it to start a new life. New identities. Somewhere far away from this place where no one knows who we are. There, no one will know who Owen is and he won't owe anyone any debts."

She looks up into my eyes and I watch as the irises of hers flicker in the sunlight. "And you won't owe anyone any debts either, huh?" she asks.

I shrug. "If they say I owe them something, then maybe I do. Though, I believe I paid my debts a long time ago."

She looks away from me.

"Why is this a bad plan?" I ask. "What's keeping you from saying yes?"

Whipping her head around to face me, she narrows her eyes. "You want to know the truth, Nicholas?" she asks.

I nod.

"I think you're lying to me."

My heart sinks into the pit of my stomach.

I swallow.

Hard.

"About what?" I ask.

"I don't know. Are you lying to me?"

"No." I shake my head.

I lift her chin upward and press my lips onto hers.

She tries to pull away but I pull her closer.

After a moment, she kisses me back.

17

OLIVE

WHEN HE KISSES ME...

*a*t first, I pull away.

I don't want him to kiss me because there is so much more that we need to talk about.

But the longer our mouths are on each other's, the more I'm reminded of the way things were when we first met.

The fire that seemed to go out during all of that time when I was waiting for Owen in the hospital suddenly gets reignited.

His hands make their way up and down my body and my head starts to swim. I forget all of the millions of thoughts that course through my mind and just let a more primal part of me take over.

He starts to undress me.

My knees start to buckle but I adjust my stance.

The room, which already felt hot is now sweltering.

My breaths speed up.

"Tell me to stop," he whispers in my ear.

His words catch me by surprise and I laugh. He laughs along with me.

"Never," I say, kissing him on the neck.

His hands tug at my clothes and he slides his hand underneath my shirt. HIs fingers feel warm against my skin but shivers still run down my spine.

I look up at him.

Our eyes lock.

When he blinks, I see that fleck of gold in his iris.

I don't want him to stop and I know that he doesn't want to stop either.

It wasn't that long ago that we were in each other's arms yet it also feels like it has been more than a century.

A strand of his hair falls into my eyes.

My mouth runs dry.

I blow the strand away just as Nicholas kisses me again.

After pulling my shirt over my head, he runs his fingers down my arm.

It tickles and I smile.

"Tell me to keep going," he whispers.

"Keep going," I reply.

In the bedroom, we lie down on the bed.

I watch the way his collarbones move slightly with each exhalation.

Propping his head, he looks at my naked breasts and draws little circles on them with his finger.

I lick my lips.

My breathing speeds up.

He puts his hand over my chest to feel my pounding heartbeat. Then he presses his ear to it.

I watch him listen to me until my breathing stabilizes. Then he turns his face and kisses me.

Pressing his lips onto my lips energizes my whole body. Goose bumps run down my skin and my nipples harden.

A fire that was barely a flame before begins to roar inside of my core. My legs open on their own.

My hips don't listen. They move up and down according to their own tempo.

We lose the rest of our clothes. Who takes off what and when, I have no idea, but a few moments later we are lying naked next to each other.

Nicholas drapes his body on top of mine.

I flex my toes.

My whole body is burning for him and I need to keep the anticipation simmering. I pull him closer.

I press my mouth on his.

"I want you inside of me...now," I whisper, biting his earlobe.

"Your request is my command," he whispers back. I open wide and welcome him inside.

"You are so beautiful," he says over and over again.

He is the sexiest man I've ever seen but I am too consumed by the moment to say a word.

The muscles in his back expand and contract with each move. Digging my hands into his flesh, I pull him deeper inside of me.

"I..." I start to say.

The words get caught in the back of my throat. He doesn't hear me but it doesn't matter.

I know what I almost said.

I love you.

The sentence is so pure and so simple. Yet, when I open my mouth again, nothing comes out.

"Are you okay?" Nicholas asks, looking down at me.

"Yes, I'm fine." I force a smile.

"Is this okay?" He double checks.

I kiss him and start to move my hips. "This is a lot more than okay," I whisper, kissing his neck.

————

"DON'T LIE TO ME, Nicholas. I...care a lot about you and I really don't want you to lie to me."

The word *care* is supposed to be *love* but I can't bring myself to say it. That kind of honesty still escapes me. But the request is true.

I wait for a moment for him to say it to me but, of course, he doesn't. Instead, he sits up and props himself up against the headboard.

The sheet lays low on his body, just below his toned pelvic region. All six of his stomach muscles relax and contract with each breath, mesmerizing me for a moment.

My own body is so much less perfect than his is and yet he looks at me exactly with the same adoration as I do at him.

"I'm not lying to you," he promises over and over again.

Yet, that feeling in the bottom of my stomach doesn't subside. It just gets more nauseating.

"So, what's the plan?" I ask, getting out of bed. "How would this whole thing work?"

"I'm glad you asked." Nicholas' eyes light up. "There's an older couple who live in a five-bedroom, five-thousand square foot home in Martha's Vineyard. They have been collecting paintings for a while and have a number in their possession. They are not particularly keen on providence."

I give him a slight nod.

That's good, I think to myself. It's not good to steal but it's better to steal from other thieves.

"Did they steal this one?"

"No, they don't steal," Nicholas says.

I bite the inside of my cheek.

"But they have no problem buying off the black market," he says. "I don't know where this painting came from, but I do know that they did not pay the fair market value for it."

I can't help but laugh. Fair market value? In the art world? Where everything is based on perception and scandal and who knows who and who will pay what?

"Something funny?" Nicholas asks. I catch myself and give him a casual shrug.

"No, not really. Just from what I've heard about the art world, they like to blow up the value of the work, somewhat."

I downplay it as much as I can but I know that I've slipped up.

"Have you ever done this before?" Nicholas asks.

"No," I say quickly.

"Never?" he pushes.

"No." I stand my ground.

I don't know why I'm not telling him the truth. It happened so long ago. But no one has ever asked me this question before. And if I were to tell anyone, it would be Nicholas Crawford. He looks into my eyes and waits. I stare back and purse my lips.

"Why do you think I have all of this experience stealing paintings?" I ask, half laughing. "You got some file on me somewhere?"

"No, not at all," he says. "Just wondering."

"So, tell me more about this job."

He goes over the basic details of the plan.

There's a vault downstairs in their wine closet, somewhere behind the bottles where they keep their most valuable paintings.

His aim is to steal this one for his client, the name of whom he refuses to give me.

"What about the rest?" I ask.

"That's where it can get a bit more interesting."

"How so?" I ask even though we both know the answer.

One option is that we do just the job that the client asked us. The client pays us one hundred grand and that's it.

The other option is to take something else as well and sell them ourselves.

That's what would set all of us up for good.

No more jobs.

No more clients.

No more stalkers or debts.

Nicholas refuses to tell me but he doesn't have as much money as he claims.

It's not tied up anywhere, it just doesn't exist.

I thought I would be mad finding this out.

But now I just internalize the information and let it wash over me.

He may not have the money now but he's a man who has certain skills and that means that he won't be broke for long.

That's probably why I'm not that angry at him.

Or perhaps it's because I've kept my own share of secrets and I know what it feels like to just want to keep something to yourself.

"You want to take other paintings, too, huh?" I ask.

He gives me a wink.

"It would really be nice to have someone in on this job who knows a thing or two about stealing artwork," he says.

I flip my hair over and toss it to give it some volume and free it of the tangles. Running my fingers through it, I smooth it over and look away from the mirror and back at him.

"Yeah, it would," I finally say.

Our eyes lock for a few moments.

He's insinuating something.

I refuse to engage.

He won't tell me he loves me.

I won't tell him I love him.

He won't tell me that he doesn't have any money.

I won't tell him about my past stealing paintings.

"So, are you in?" Nicholas asks.

18

OLIVE
WHEN WE MAKE A COMPROMISE...

I think about it for a moment. I don't want to *want to* do this but it would be a lie if I'd say I didn't.

Suddenly, I have an itch to scratch again.

But this offer is also more than that. This would be a way out. This would be enough money for all of us to disappear. Together!

Now, that's an idea! The only person who doesn't need a reason to flee is me and yet if I want to keep both Owen and Nicholas in my life, going away together is the only way.

Nicholas has it all planned out.

I ask him to go over the details twice just to make sure that they all sound right.

The thing about coming up with these kind of plans is to think of all the things that can go wrong.

It's not enough to just lay out the steps of what to do, you also have to lay out the steps of everything you would do if a hundred other things happened preventing you from doing the thing you planned on doing.

"We need Owen," I say.

"Does that mean you're in?" Nicholas' eyes light up.

"I'm in if he's in."

He's not happy to hear this.

I'm not surprised.

"Okay, hear me out. We need a third person and we're doing this partly for him. So, what's the point of sharing in the loot with a stranger when he is the one who would benefit?"

"That's hard to argue with him," he says after a moment.

I let out a sigh of relief.

"But I'll give it a try," Nicholas adds. "Owen hates my guts."

I wait for him to say more, but he doesn't.

"So?"

"So? Is that not enough?"

I inhale deeply.

"No, it's not," I finally say. "In most cases, it would be, but not this one."

"Why?"

"Don't you see that I'm stuck in the middle here? He's my brother and you're my boyfriend. You two have reasons to disappear, I don't. But if I want to keep you in my life, both of you, we have to disappear together. All three of us."

He looks at me as if I'm saying something ridiculous when we both know that he has thought about this a number of times before.

"You could disappear by yourself and he could also and you would never to have to deal with one another again, but if you want me then we have to do this thing together."

Nicholas rubs his temples and stares out into the distance, somewhere past me.

"He's not really your brother," he says after a moment.

"That doesn't change our history. It doesn't change the way I feel about him."

"It changes the way he feels about you, Olive. He's in love with you."

"I don't care about that," I say quickly, trying to change the topic. "He hasn't said anything to me about it and he's nothing but my brother in my eyes."

Shaking his head, Nicholas makes his hands into fists until the whites of his knuckles appear.

I leave it at that for now. As long as he is not outwardly rejecting the proposition, it's good enough for me. Now, I have another problem to deal with: convincing Owen to get on board.

———

THAT AFTERNOON, I meet Owen in a bookstore. I haven't been to a bookstore in ages and have forgotten how much I missed the smell of paper and the feel of it under my fingertips.

It was his suggestion to meet here and I get here half an hour early to browse through the selections.

There is nothing like getting lost in a bookstore.

I make my way slowly through the aisles, picking up books by authors I had forgotten and judging the books, not only by their covers but also by the size of the print and the texture of the pages.

I look up some of my favorite authors, the

ones I've discovered on Amazon, but of course they are nowhere to be found.

Since all of them are independently published, few if any of the chain bookstores stock the titles. That's probably why so few ebook readers don't bother with going to real bookstores anymore. Why would they?

It's unfortunate really because those readers read two or more books a week.

Still, I find the outing satisfying.

I lose myself in the blurb by a female author I've never heard of before and am pleased when the words on the first page flow easily and rapidly to keep me turning to the next, and the one after that.

"Hey, I was looking for you," Owen says, bumping into my shoulder and breaking me out of my deep trance.

As I close the book, keeping my finger in between the pages where I stopped reading, the lights above my head seem to grow in intensity along with the humdrum noises around me.

"Kind of lost myself in this for a bit," I admit.

"Totally get it," Owen says, showing me his haul of three rather imposing hardbacks.

"Is that what you're getting?" I ask, becoming keenly aware of the cost of buying these hardcovers in this store.

I'm tempted to quickly look up the prices on my phone and order him the books from Amazon but I fight the urge.

I'm not going to be one of *those* people. We found the books in this store, so we're going to pay the prices set out by them.

Not doing so would lead to the exact problem that's taking place everywhere in America; the closing of all the bookstores in lieu of people only online shopping for books.

"Can I buy you a cup of coffee?" I ask. "I need to talk to you about something."

19

OLIVE

WHEN WE ARGUE...

The sound of the machine milling coffee beans irks me as we stand in line behind a couple of chatty teenage girls.

Owen gives me a warm smile as he asks me if I have read any good books lately.

I tilt my head and let out a little shrug.

I hate to admit it but I am a little embarrassed to tell him what I've been reading.

Even though romance books are some of the most popular books on the planet there is a big stigma associated with them. Even those who enjoy them often refer to them as trashy or some other demeaning adjective.

There was a time when I thought that myself. There was a time when I only read books by critically acclaimed writers and those that have been approved by the gatekeepers in the publishing industry.

But then I stumbled upon a whole other world of fiction that I never knew existed.

In this place, writers weren't censored by editors and publishers and just wrote and published books that they wanted.

Some left much to be desired but others surpassed all of my expectations.

Owen and I have talked about a lot of things during his time in prison but we haven't talked about this.

After ordering a latte, I rattle off a list of books I've never mentioned to him before.

"Oh, I've never heard of them before," he says. "Can I find them here?"

I shake my head and explain that those books can only be found online.

Pulling out my phone, I show him the covers.

There are some with objects and landscapes but the majority of them are graced by shirtless men.

Owen starts to laugh.

"Okay, I wouldn't have shown this to you if I thought that you would make fun of me."

By his demeanor, I know that he clearly doesn't understand how difficult it was for me to come out and share.

I kick myself for bringing it up in the first place.

I am here to convince him to do something he won't want to do and instead of creating an atmosphere that would be conducive to him saying yes, I am throwing up obstacles.

"C'mon, Olive," Owen says when we take a seat in the cafe. "Maybe those books are your guilty pleasure but you don't actually read them the way you would read real literature."

This statement makes my blood run hot.

My cheeks get flushed and my eyes narrow.

"You have no idea what you're talking about, Owen," I say through my teeth. "Those books are just as good as any of the ones you read. And just because they have some shirtless men on the covers doesn't mean that they are my guilty pleasure."

"Fine," he says, throwing his hands up. "I didn't mean for you to get offended."

Standing up, I push my chair back.

It makes a loud squeaking sound against the tile floor and everyone around us looks up.

"I don't need this...judgement from you," I whisper and walk toward the front door.

I'm fuming and my hands are balled up in fists.

I am halfway down the block before Owen catches up with me.

The blood is pounding so loudly in my head that I only hear him calling my name when he grabs my shoulder and swings me around.

"Olive, I'm sorry. I'm really sorry."

Tears that have been welling up in my eyes suddenly break free and run down my cheeks.

They have little to do with the scene in the bookstore and more with all of the stress that I have been under over these last few weeks.

The last few sleepless nights also haven't helped matters in terms of regulating my emotional state.

"Oh my God, Olive." Owen pulls me into his arms. "I'm so sorry. I didn't mean it. I'm so sorry."

His words are muffled by my sobs.

I let him hold me for a bit before finally getting the strength to pull away.

"No, I'm so stupid. This has nothing to do with that. I'm just feeling really...fragile with everything that's going on."

"Still, I shouldn't have said those things. Reading is so personal and the things that connect with you are different from the things that speak to me. The kind of books we read are intertwined with our own lives and the experiences that we've gone through. I had no right to say those things to you."

For some reason, his apology makes my tears rush out at an even faster rate.

I keep wiping them away, but they just don't let up.

"This has nothing to do with you," I mumble, rubbing my eyes with the back of my hands. "I feel so dumb. Why can't I stop crying?"

Owen lifts my chin up and cradles my face in his palms.

He gazes into my eyes and I suddenly start to feel better.

He sees me for who I am. All of those letters during all of those years were not for naught.

The connection between us is real.

And then suddenly, something shifts.

It's hard to explain exactly but it's as if he's no longer looking at me like a brother does at a sister.

There's a new depth in our gaze.

It's the first time that I feel like he wants something more from me. I pull away.

After that my eyes dry quickly.

He looks down at his shoes and shuffles his feet. It occurs to me that my mom was telling me the truth.

Owen does have feelings for me that go beyond what we have as siblings.

I bite my lower lip, trying to decide how to fix this mess that I have created.

I should've just come right out and told him what I needed to tell him.

We don't have much time and we definitely don't have time to deal with something this complicated.

No, the best thing is to put this away.

I don't dare talk about it and bring it into the light.

I need him to help us do the job and I need him to run away with us. If I let him bring up how he really feels about me then it's going to ruin everything.

20

OLIVE
WHEN I ASK HIM...

The fresh cool air clears my head and forces me to collect my thoughts. Owen keeps trying to talk about what happened in the bookstore.

I force myself to genuinely accept his apology and then quickly steer the conversation to something else.

"Let's take a walk, I need to talk to you about something," I say and start to walk.

It's a plaza like any other. A bunch of chain big box stores with sprawling parking lots out front.

A park would have been a better option but to get to one we have to get back in the car.

No, this will do.

Some people walk purposely to the stores from their cars and others are pushing large carts overloaded with bags toward theirs.

We are completely out in public but no one will hear us because they aren't here to listen.

I don't know exactly where to start but I don't want to wait any longer. I simply jump in.

"I need your help," I say.

Owen nods and waits for me to continue. I take a deep breath and lay out the plan.

He listens carefully, burying his hands in the pockets of his jacket.

"You think we should run away?" he asks. "Together."

I had laid out the plan with some of the general details, and only mentioned this part of it briefly, but this is of course the one thing he focuses on.

"Don't you?" I say. "They tried to kill you once. They'll do it again."

Owen clears his throat.

"What about Mom?" he asks.

I shake my head.

His question makes me angry.

She hardly visited him in prison or in the hospital, but she remains his first consideration when making decisions about his life.

But saying any of this out loud is not going to make convincing him to do this any easier.

"What about your life?" I pivot. "You have to get out of here if you want to stay alive. At least, for a while."

He shrugs.

"We can tell Mom later. You can reach out and tell her that you're fine but not where you are. For her safety. In case anyone comes to her place looking for you."

Owen stops walking and taps his toe on the ground again, thinking.

"What if we went together?" he asks, looking up at me with his big wide eyes.

My body tenses up.

He's not looking at me like a brother again, but I try to brush this feeling off.

"I can't go with you and leave Nicholas," I say sternly.

"Why?"

"He's my boyfriend and I love him."

Unlike before, the word 'love' comes out easily and without much fanfare. It takes me by surprise but Owen does not notice.

"C'mon, Olive. Really? You're going to spend the rest of your life with him?"

"I don't know what's going to happen in the future," I admit. "But I am with him now and I want it that way."

I wish this wasn't so complicated.

A part of me wants to just run away with Nicholas and forget all about Owen and my fucked up family.

For a moment, I'm tempted to suggest something unthinkable.

What if we got some money and then he used it to disappear on his own? He could start a new life somewhere.

Meet a nice girl.

Fall in love.

Maybe have kids.

No one would ever have to know that he ever served time.

That could be his new break. But staring into his dark eyes, I know that if I were to say this out loud, it would break him.

He doesn't want to start a new life somewhere because that would mean he would be away from me.

If I don't go with him, he won't go.

He won't see a reason to go and then they're going to hurt him.

The truth is that despite the fact that we're not related, Owen is my family. I couldn't live with myself knowing that I didn't do everything in my power to protect him.

"You need to help us do this," I say as firmly as possible. "We need another person and everything we get is going to benefit you directly so you are the best man for this job. Afterward, we will have enough money to set us up for life. We will start new identities. And you'll be able to help Mom more than you can now. But most importantly, you'll be able to get away from *them*."

Owen moves his jaw from one side of his face to the other as he mulls over my proposal. "What about my parole?"

"That's the thing," I say. "If you run away, they'll put a warrant out for your arrest. And if they catch you, they'll send you back to prison."

"That doesn't sound great," he admits.

"But if they don't catch you then you'll never have to check in with a parole officer again. You'll be a free man, starting now."

I can't believe that I'm advocating for this but it's the only way out.

"If you stay in Boston, you risk getting killed. If you do this job and run away then you only risk going back to prison."

"That's quite a conundrum," he says after a moment.

"You know that I wouldn't be suggesting this if I thought you had another way out."

We turn into an alley between Walmart and Bed Bath & Beyond.

The wind picks up and we put our backs against the towering, windowless wall. A lone car drives in front of us, slowing down briefly at the stop sign.

"How much money are we talking about here?" Owen asks.

When I turn to face him, I see a big smile spread on his face.

21

NICHOLAS

I find it hard to believe that Owen has actually agreed to do this job with us even as I wait here for them to arrive.

The room I rented is a three-star unassuming no frills hotel aimed at middle management business professionals who spend a lot of their time in airports.

There is no bulletproof plexiglass downstairs but there's also no concierge service.

The lobby is small and furnished in vinyl and the coffee is stale and cold.

The room is nice enough but there is no bellman or room service. I take a seat on the couch next to the bed and flip on the television.

I cringe at the noise that couch makes whenever I make even the slightest move and tap my fingers on my lap.

When she knocks, I jump out of my seat and only then realize exactly how nervous I am about this.

I take a deep breath before I open the door to calm myself down. This won't work if you don't act like you can do this in your sleep.

"Come in." I fling the door open and quickly turn away from them.

I hurry back to the dining room table next to the couch and bury myself in the paperwork that I had spread out on it.

"Thanks for coming," I say, picking up the top sheet and examining it closely.

I got all of the plans directly from Art and none of them needed to be written out.

But in order to make it seem like they all came from my own research, I have made copious notes full of crossed out parts and annotations.

Olive glances over my work and picks up a few sheets to examine them more closely.

"I can't read this," she announces.

Since they are not meant to be read, I smile on the inside.

Owen throws himself onto the couch and it explodes in a cacophony of high-pitched squeaking, which doesn't seem to bother him a bit.

"Nice place," he says without a tinge of irony.

"Thanks." I nod. "And thanks for coming."

"I'm here to hear you out. That's it."

This takes me by surprise. I straighten my shoulders and adjust my stance.

"What?" I ask Olive.

She doesn't say anything so I look at him.

Another blank stare.

"I thought that you were down to do this," I finally say.

"No, I need to hear the plan first."

I shake my head.

"What's wrong?" Olive asks.

"That's not going to happen," I say, shaking my head.

"Why?" he asks.

"You can't hear the plan without committing to this...project first."

"I can't commit to this project unless you have a sound plan."

"I have a sound plan. All of my plans are sound," I insist.

"Do you want me to be a part of this?" Owen asks, standing up.

"No, not really," I say. "But if you're going to be getting any of the money, I think you should contribute."

"You know what?" he says, taking a step toward me.

Instead of backing away, I take another step toward him.

"Yeah, what?" I raise my voice.

"I don't need this. I don't need you."

"And I don't need you either. I'm doing *you* a favor, man!"

"Fuck you!" He takes a step to the side and then slams his shoulder in mine.

The anger that has been boiling right below the surface suddenly explodes. I make a fist and punch him in the nose.

He winces in pain and when he pulls his hand away from his face, I see that it's covered in blood.

"Aggh!" he yells and launches himself at me.

The force of his body pushes me to the floor and I land on my back.

A second later, the first punch collides with my head.

Then another and another.

The wind gets temporarily knocked out of me and my chest constricts as I struggle to breathe.

I hear a high voice screaming somewhere around us but her words are muffled by the ringing in between my ears.

Somehow, I manage to push him off me and throw myself on top of him.

I punch him a few times and my hand feels good colliding with his face.

After a few more, my fingers start to throb but I keep at it.

Olive's voice starts to come in more clearly but I still don't really process what she's saying.

"Get off him!" she screams into my ear just as she hits me with something hard.

My head starts to spin and my body gets wobbly.

I try to move off Owen but instead I just melt onto the floor.

"You were going to kill him." I hear her say when my eyes open and I manage to focus on her face. "You both were going to kill each other."

My head is throbbing and I'm lying on the bed.

She keeps going over what happened as if I wasn't there or as if it's going to make me feel better.

Owen is lying on the couch with his hand over his face.

Like most physical altercations, our fight has resolved nothing but it did allow us to blow off some steam.

We both got a bunch of good punches in.

My throbbing face and right hand are a testament to that.

With us on our backs, Olive takes charge.

"This isn't going to work unless we all cooperate," she says, standing in the middle of the floor. "We all need each other."

"I am not starting any new life with that asshole," Owen mumbles.

My chest tightens.

He doesn't need me as much as I need him, but my only consolation is that neither of them know this.

If I can get this painting then I won't have to work for the FBI anymore gathering evidence on him and I won't have to worry about paying off any debts that the mob thinks I owe them.

Of course, I can do this on my own and disappear but I want Olive to come with me. And the only way she'll do that is if she can bring Owen along.

I know all of this and I have gone over it a million times already. I keep looking for a way out but nothing presents itself.

"I'm ready to talk about this whenever you are, Olive," I say, forcing myself to my feet.

My body throbs and aches but I don't dare let out a sound.

My announcement catches Owen's attention.

Now he looks like the uncooperative one.

Now he looks like the asshole that I know that he is.

"What's the plan?" Olive asks.

I walk over to the dining room table and pick up my scribbled notes.

I'm about to open my mouth when I remember the promise that Owen still owes me.

"I can't get into any of these details without him committing to do this job with us," I say as calmly as possible.

22

NICHOLAS

WHEN WE BEGIN AGAIN…

I address my words to Olive.

She's the one who is in the middle.

She's the mediator who can make this happen. I turn to face her and wait.

It's her turn now. She walks over to Owen who sits up on the couch with an angry yet defeated look on his face.

He crosses his arms and legs, withdrawing himself as much as possible from everything around him.

I want to give them some space but there's nowhere to go. I take a few steps away and then disappear into the bathroom. With the light on and the fan running, I can't hear what they're saying.

But when I come out, there's the beginning of a smile at the corners of Olive's mouth. I let out a small sigh of relief.

Without insisting on an apology or an explanation, I accept his nod as a sign that he's in.

"The couple who own the painting are in their late sixties. They live in a five-bedroom, five-thousand square foot home in Martha's Vineyard. They have a number of paintings in their collection," I say.

"How did they get into that?" Olive asks.

"I'm not sure. The husband worked in a hedge fund and the wife was in the upper echelons of a big pharmaceutical company. They both retired with millions."

"Have you done anything like this before?" Owen asks.

His words are jagged and rude but I choose to ignore the tone.

"No, I've never taken a painting before," I say calmly.

"What makes you think you can do it then?" He pushes me.

"Owen, please," Olive interjects. "I want to hear the plan."

"Even though Mr. and Mrs. Linchfield are rich, they did not buy these paintings from reputable art dealers or galleries."

Olive stares at me with a look of surprise.

"The paintings are stolen and they bought them from their contacts in the black market," I continue.

"Is that who is paying you?" Olive asks. "The people they stole the painting from?"

I swallow hard.

That's exactly what Art says Olive did and it would be too much of a coincidence if this story went the same way.

"No." I shake my head. "I don't think so."

The story is not all true but it's true enough to get Olive on my side.

They wait for me to continue.

I try to think of the best way to organize and present the details that Art gave me.

"The painting we want is called Dark Blue Mirror by Alexandra Blur," I continue. "It's basically a large canvas that's all dark blue."

I pull up the painting on my phone and show it to them. Its website lists it to be estimated at seven-hundred thousand dollars.

"Wait a second," Owen says. "Seven hundred for this? Just some blue paint the whole way around and that's it?"

I tilt my head to one side.

"That's the art world, Owen," Olive says.

"But that doesn't make any sense!"

"Well, that's how it is." She shrugs. "I don't know what to tell you."

"So, can I paint this and get that much money?" he asks, incensed.

"No." She laughs.

"Why the hell not?"

"Because...you're not an artist. You're not saying anything."

"There are people starving in the world, working hundreds of hours just to put food on the table and someone is spending this kind of money on this shit?"

I hate to admit it but he does have a point.

I don't know much about the modern art world but the prices there for the quality of the work are outrageous.

It doesn't seem to have anything to do with the painting but rather the painter and the valuation for the investors.

"It's just like the housing market," Olive says. "Ten years ago houses cost two hundred grand and now they're six. The market deems it so, so that's what happens."

"Okay, I'll give you that," Owen says. "But they're still fucking houses, Olive. They're not a huge canvas painted one color. There's some value in that you can live in them."

He waits for her to say something else but she just throws up her hands.

"Am I wrong?" Owen asks. "I mean, really, am I wrong?"

Again, she doesn't say anything.

"Nicholas?" Owen asks, extending me an olive branch, the first one since I've known him.

"It's fucking ridiculous," I agree.

"Thank you! That's all I wanted to hear."

"But it doesn't mean that it's not worth that," I say. "And that we're not going to get a nice chunk of cash when we take it."

"I'm not saying that at all. I just wanted to hear that I'm not crazy for thinking that that's an outrageous amount of money to pay for something like that."

This conversation lightens the mood a bit and we manage a few smiles.

I continue to go over the details, which are a lot more general than I would've wanted.

Art promised me that he's going to take care of all of the planning, but the problem is that he thinks giving me the address and the location of their safe is enough.

As I relay everything I know about the plan, Olive quickly decides that it's not enough and that we must do more research.

Tempted to fight her on it, I decide against it.

I am not doing this job on official FBI business and if we were to get caught then Art would wash his hands of me.

Olive is the only one with real art theft experience so if she thinks we need to do more prep work then that's what we'll do.

23

OLIVE

WHEN WE GET READY…

*T*he Linchfield house is located at the end of a cul-de-sac on a street with only three other houses.

The lots are wide and expansive filled with thick vegetation that walls them off from their neighbors.

At first, I thought we would have to contend with gates and guards but neither are present there.

There are also no neighbors in sight.

I have staked out this house for a few days and I haven't seen a single other person coming or going on this street.

Martha's Vineyard is known to be a summer playground for rich New Yorkers but the isolation on this street takes even me by surprise.

I am tempted to think that this will be a much easier job than I had originally imagined it to be, but I don't dare allow myself to get complacent or lazy.

Stealing almost three quarters of a million dollars' worth of art is not something anyone should take lightly.

After the initial fight in that hotel room, Owen and Nicholas seem to be getting along quite well.

Owen is behaving himself. He hasn't made any of his usual under-his-breath remarks.

I appreciate it more than he'll probably ever know but I hate choosing sides and being stuck in the middle of them.

We planned the robbery for this evening, during sunset.

The painting is large and we will need a car to get it out of the area.

But out of fear of being spotted, I decided that Owen should wait for us away from here.

It's not so late that it would look suspicious for Owen to sit in the van with Thompson's Plumbing on the side.

In case anyone asks him, he will play the role of a frustrated plumber frantically talking on the phone to get parts that should have arrived already.

He will wait for us in the driveway of an empty house one street over and we will carry the painting down the ravine between the two houses and right into his van.

The plan isn't flawless.

I wish I knew exactly what kind of safe the Linchfields have and had more time to think of possible problems that could come up.

Unfortunately, the owners are coming home this weekend and we are out of time.

After going over the plans late into the night, we review them a few more times on the drive over.

Everyone seems ready on the outside.

We are all properly caffeinated with empty bladders and stoic faces.

Trembling on the inside, I hide my nervousness behind a layer of workout clothes and bury my unsteady hands in the pockets of my hoodie.

Owen is dressed in a Thompson Plumbing uniform with a fake name embroidered on the front.

The shop wasn't going to have it ready until tomorrow but with a bit of prodding and a one-hundred dollar tip, the snotty teenager manning the desk was able to miraculously finish it in time.

When I handed him the shirt this morning, I avoided going into the details.

The exorbitant tip would get him all hung up and he'd focus his grudge against the eleventh grader instead of the task at hand.

Owen circles around the cul-de-sac, slowing down only briefly for Nicholas and me to open the door and slide out.

We rush to the back of the house, knowing that the owners of the two adjacent homes won't be here for another two months.

Still, you can never be too careful.

I run our cover story in my head over and over again in case anyone does stop us.

We are training for the 10k Wild run, a local race taking place in two weeks that requires contestants to run ten kilometers in the woods and over uneven ground. The ravine behind the Linchfield's house is the perfect training space.

Nicholas picks the lock on the back door. It only takes him a few seconds wiggling the metal tool to get it unlocked.

Now, it's my turn.

I have inspected the door before and I know that the security system that they use is magnetic.

It's a small metal box and the sensor has two parts.

One is stationary and the other is attached to the movable part of the door.

The idea is that when the magnetic connection between the two parts of the sensor are broken, the alarm activates.

I pull a magnet that I bought at a nearby dollar store out of my pocket.

It's a smiley face emoji refrigerator magnet but it should do the trick.

I slide the magnet over the sensor through the tiny slit in the door frame.

Once it attaches, I hold my breath and open the door. A wave of relief washes over me when the alarm doesn't go off.

"Good job," Nicholas whispers.

The door leads us to a spacious Mediterranean-style kitchen with a big hood and thick bricks lining the stove.

Near the dining room, we find the staircase that goes downstairs.

The steps are covered in carpet as is the rest of the basement, consisting of three rooms.

The owners use the first room as a home theater and there are large overstuffed recliners facing a seventy-inch, wall-mounted television.

One of the rooms leading off this one is a bedroom and another is the office.

"Here it is!" Nicholas yells while I briefly lose myself in the small five by eight painting on the wall in front of the enormous oak desk.

It has to be a replica, right?

I take a few steps closer to it and peer into the piece. The work isn't so much a painting as a plan for a painting.

There are a few brush strokes made in oil but the rest of it is in pencil. The artist was making plans for what's to come.

"Olive, we don't have all day," he calls me from the other room.

A moment later, he appears in the doorway.

"What are you doing?"

"This...this can't be real," I whisper.

"What do you mean?"

I grab my phone and look up his work on Google, confirming my suspicions.

"This is by Claude Monet. It's an early version or a proposal for his famous Waterlilies in Bloom painting," I whisper. "At least, I think so."

Nicholas stares at the picture for a moment. "We have to open that safe," he finally says.

I nod.

He's right.

We're here to get that painting and I shouldn't be sidetracked. On the other hand, the one in the safe is worth seven-hundred grand on the real market, probably around four hundred on the black one, and this one, if it's real, is worth millions.

But it can't be real, right?

Why would it just be hanging here on the wall without much more than a piece of glass protecting it from the outside world?

"Show me the safe," I say, forcing myself away from the Monet.

24

OLIVE
WHEN WE GET TO THE SAFE...

*T*he safe is located in the closet of the bedroom. It's hidden from view by a stack of old clothing and coats.

It would be hard to find if Nicholas' contact hadn't told him about its exact whereabouts.

I am slightly relieved by the fact that the safe looks older than I had expected.

I brought a few different tools because I wasn't sure what kind of safe it was going to be and this one would require a drill.

I lay my running backpack on the floor and pull out the drill.

"You know what you're doing, right?"
Nicholas asks.

I narrow my eyes, clearly annoyed.

These kind of statements do little to instill confidence, and confidence is exactly what I'm lacking right about now.

I feel around the safe and knock to listen for changes in design.

The hollow parts sound different from the rest.

I reach for the door and tug it for a moment, hoping for the best. Sometimes when the owner forgets to lock the safe, simply turning it gets it open.

I wouldn't want to be the kind of robber to pass up a simple opportunity like that.

Unfortunately, the safe is indeed locked.

I take a deep breath and press the drill bit to the metal door.

The method is simple enough but there are a number of risks to this approach.

Many modern high security safes use thick plates to prevent drilling. If you were to drill into one of these barrier materials the collision with the drill will destroy the bit.

I brought a number of additional drill bits of various hardness but I have no way of knowing the strength of the barrier plates until I actually start drilling.

Another thing to worry about is the glass re-locker.

Practically every safe worth its price now uses a glass sheet right below the spring loaded re-locking bars to automatically lock the safe in case of this exact situation.

In order to prevent the glass re-locker from activating, I have to drill slowly and carefully, listening for any irregularity in the wall.

The first drill bit breaks almost immediately.

The second snaps just as fast.

The third one quickly follows.

I've brought backups of each hardness but I keep going up in hardness hoping that the next one will do the job.

When the fifth one finally starts to drill, I let out a slight sigh of relief.

"What's wrong?" Nicholas asks when I stop drilling for a moment.

"Shh." I put the drill down for a second and press my index finger to my lips.

When our eyes meet, I see the perspiration on his forehead, but I don't let his worries cloud my thinking.

I pick up the drill again and line up the bit with the hole.

Before I turn it on, I tap it a few times trying to figure out whether I'm in danger of hitting glass.

To tell the truth, I am uncertain.

The sound is loud and piercing but it doesn't mean that it's necessarily glass.

When I'm about to press to start the drill again, Nicholas' voice startles me.

"Someone's here," he whispers, reading a text on his phone. "He thought she was just looking around the house but she's probably going in."

Shit, shit, shit, I whisper silently while Nicholas reverberates my thoughts out loud.

Without wasting a moment, I press the drill into the hole and start it up again and pray that I don't hit glass. A moment later, I pull the door open and peer inside.

Nicholas pulls out a round tube, popping the top open.

He pulls out the rolled canvas to confirm that it is indeed the Dark Blue Mirror by Alexandra Blur that we are looking for.

With people's footsteps above our heads we don't have any time to debate whether this collection of blue brushstrokes is worth the price tag.

When Nicholas slides the painting back into its tube, I quickly pack my tools back into my backpack.

Hearing the creak in the door leading to the basement, I hold my breath.

Nicholas quickly shuts the door to the safe, buries it behind the clothes in the closet, and pushes us in the opposite corner.

If someone were to open the door, they'd have to be really looking for us to notice a thing.

We wait.

Footsteps come downstairs.

I hold my breath.

The pounding of my heart sounds like a war zone in my head. Nicholas grabs my hand and squeezes it tightly.

We wait.

We didn't bring any weapons because we have no intention of making this violent.

Yet at the same time we did not really give much thought to what we would do in this situation.

If anyone were to see us, I always thought it would be on the outside.

A neighbor perhaps?

Or maybe a friend stopping by to check on the place?

I don't know who this person is but her footsteps are light and meticulous.

She is looking for something. We hold our breaths. Silently, I pray that whatever she's searching for, it will not be inside the closet where we both stand pressed against the wall.

She reaches for the closet door.

My heart jumps into my throat. Nicholas squeezes my hand even tighter and we continue to wait.

I still have no plan as to what to do if she were to find us. My only hope is that Nicholas does.

The handle of the door rotates and I wait for the inevitable.

Except that it doesn't come.

I open my eyes and peer into the darkness.

I can't see the handle but I hear it snap back into place.

One footstep follows another except that now they are getting further and further away.

I don't let myself let out a sigh of relief until she gets all the way to the top of the landing and slams the basement door shut behind her.

"Who was that?" I whisper, my words barely audible.

"No idea," Nicholas whispers back.

When he lets go of my hand, a wave of relief rushes over me.

But we're not out of danger yet.

We're still in a closet in a strange house.

Nicholas looks down at his phone. Owen's text shines brightly in the dark.

When he clicks on it, we both read the words on the screen: *she's gone.*

25

NICHOLAS
WHEN WE GET OUT…

My heartbeat doesn't stop pounding until we get out of the house, run through the ravine, and up the other side.

In fact, it doesn't really return to its normal beat until Owen pulls out of the housing development and then onto the highway.

He drives at a regular suburban pace, careful not to draw attention to himself.

We are eager to celebrate but we don't want to tempt our luck.

"How was that?" I ask.

I adjust my seat on the plastic crate underneath my butt but it doesn't make it any softer.

"She almost walked into the closet," Olive says, turning to face Owen. "I had no idea what we were going to do if she opened it."

I insisted on not bringing a gun for that exact situation.

It's so easy to resort to deadly force when in reality it's really not needed.

If she had opened the closet, I would have rushed out past her, knocking her down to the floor and then fleeing up the stairs.

With the hoodies and sunglasses over our eyes and the simple act of surprise, the woman would have had a difficult time identifying us to the authorities.

Besides, if we were ever caught and put on trial, robbery with a deadly weapon carries a much bigger charge than burglary.

"That's why I wanted you to have a gun," Owen says.

He did not agree with me and did everything but call me a coward for wanting to prevent irreversible consequences.

But since it was Olive and me going in, the decision was hers and she sided with me.

When Olive again asks him about the woman, he just shrugs. "I have no idea. It seemed like she was a friend of the family because she just pulled up and walked in. She had a key. Maybe she was looking for something."

"Well, at least she didn't look inside the closet," Olive says.

I run my fingers over the tube with the rolled up painting laying on top of my feet.

When we hit a bump in the road, the hard edges of the frame underneath my hoodie jam into my chest.

At least, she didn't come after we left and notice that the Monet is missing from the wall, I say silently to myself.

I let that thought linger in my mind as I mull it over.

We had originally planned to take other paintings but we didn't see any on the way down.

There were also no additional paintings in the vault. And on the way out, Olive was too shaken up to consider the Monet again.

She doesn't know that I took the Monet and she doesn't know that I took some other things as well: a Rolex watch, a Cartier tennis bracelet, and a Tiffany's diamond ring that looks to be at least five carats.

But I'm not hiding any of this from Olive.

I want to show her every last piece and I want to celebrate our victory together.

Unfortunately, I can't.

The person I'm hiding these from is her brother.

I don't trust him and he doesn't trust me.

Our plan is to disappear together and then eventually live separate lives.

I'll set him up with some of the proceeds of this job, but I will not share it evenly. I will not share it three ways.

In an ideal world, he wouldn't be involved with this at all.

He wouldn't know my new identity and I'd have no ties to him.

But nothing is perfect.

He's Olive's family and until he does something to betray her, I have to accept him as part of our relationship.

But that doesn't mean that I have to share millions of dollars with him.

We drive to a large parking lot packed with cars and find a spot near the top.

An acquaintance is going to pick up the van later this evening.

When we get into my rental, I drive all of us to a suite I rented at the Marriott.

It's not the Ritz, not yet, but it's better than where we met before.

Besides, Olive's apartment is out of the question because Sydney and James are there.

I checked in earlier and we go straight to the elevator.

We are each rolling carry-on suitcases filled with changes of clothes and other supplies.

We know better than to say a word until we are inside but the half smiles on everyone's faces says it all.

I rented Owen a nearby room, at the end of the hall, which seems to satisfy him.

"Anybody want anything to drink?" I ask, heading straight to the minibar.

While Olive uses the bathroom and Owen takes off his uniform, I pull the Monet out of my hoodie and drop it carefully behind the dresser for safe keeping.

Due to their size, the watch and the jewelry are a lesser consideration and I keep them in various pockets of my clothes.

Afterward, we sit around the dining room table and celebrate with a round of beers.

I relay how much of an expert Olive is at cracking safes and how many drill bits it took to get through it.

By the time we talk through the story for the third time, we are on our second round and the level of celebration is getting bigger.

"So, how did you know how to do all of that?" Owen asks.

"I have a feeling that Olive has a lot more experience with stealing paintings than she is letting on," I say with a laugh.

"You do, right? I mean, how would you know how to do it otherwise?"

Olive stares at us, her eyes blinking at irregular intervals. This is her chance to tell the truth. What would it hurt? I wonder.

"Apparently, you two have never heard of YouTube before," she says.

"You learned how to do that on the internet?" Owen asks.

She nods.

"You'd be surprised what you can learn online."

Our eyes meet and I hold her gaze.

Why is she lying?

Why won't she just come out and tell us the truth?

My only consolation is that perhaps she doesn't want to tell Owen.

But then I remember that she had lied to me about this before as well.

"So what now?" she asks.

"I'll take the painting to my contact and he'll pay us," I say with a shrug.

"By yourself?" Owen asks.

I nod.

"Is that a problem?" I ask, my body tensing up.

"Yes, it is," he says, glaring at me.

26

OLIVE
WHEN WE MAKE FUTURE PLANS…

*T*he relief of getting away with the painting without getting caught does not last long.

I want to spend the night having a few drinks and relaxing but there is little trust between the two men in my life.

I know that Nicholas got Owen a room at the end of the hall because he wanted to give us some privacy tonight but Owen is reading nothing but suspicion into that.

"Owen, that guy is Nicholas' contact. He was always going to turn over the painting and get paid for it on his own."

Nicholas reaches for my hand under the table and gives me a knowing squeeze.

"I don't care," Owen says. "I'm not comfortable with that. That's a lot of money. A lot of my money."

"Hey, you wouldn't even be in on this deal if it weren't for her," Nicholas says. "And don't forget who we are doing all of this for."

"Oh, please, you're doing it for yourself. You don't have any fucking money and you needed Olive to help you."

"We're doing this for *you*! They're going to kill you and at this point I hope they fucking do it."

Their voices get louder and louder and my head begins to throb.

What the hell was I thinking? They're never going to get along. They are never going to have peace.

"Listen," I start to say.

"Listen to me!" I say louder. But their shouts continue.

"Shut the fuck up!" I finally scream.

They close their mouths and look at me.

"Owen, I'm not going to let anything happen to that painting. Tomorrow, Nicholas is going to give it to his contact and that's what's going to happen. I don't care if you don't like it but this is not your call."

He tries to say something in response but I cut him off.

"Now, we need to talk about what happens after. Where do we go? How do we disappear?"

"I have a guy working on our passports and driver's licenses. We will have them tomorrow along with the money. The only thing we have to do is decide where we want to go."

Owen lets out a long sigh of defeat.

"What do you mean?" he asks, finishing his beer and opening another.

I am not sure if we have avoided this topic on purpose or maybe just didn't want to press our luck in case something went wrong with the first part of the plan, but none of us have actually talked about where we would like to go to start our new lives.

Silence falls for a few moments.

I try to think of my ideal place if there is such a thing.

I never did much traveling but I've always loved the idea of it.

Being with new people, experiencing new cultures, eating new food.

But what we are about to embark on isn't exactly travel.

It's more like choosing a new place to begin a new life.

"This isn't a permanent situation," Nicholas says, reading my mind. "It's not like we have to get jobs and live undercover."

"So, we can just travel for a bit?" I ask, my voice rising at the top with the possibility.

Owen clears his throat.

Oh, yes, of course.

There are three of us in this and I doubt that he will want to tag along on a tour of Europe or Australia.

Or maybe he would?

"You did say you always wanted to see the world," I point out.

"Not a good idea," Owen says categorically.

I bite the inside of my cheek.

"Why?" I ask.

"If I disappear and don't report to my parole officer, I'm a fugitive. If they find me then they'll tack on those remaining years and I'll have to serve them in prison on top of the additional charges. The less I travel, or rather the less I use a passport for international travel, the better. Maybe it would be a good idea to travel around the US though, but I'm not sure."

I look down at my hands and twist my sterling silver infinity ring around my right ring finger.

I'm not sure what to say to him or the best way to deal with this.

"So, what are you thinking?" I ask.

He shrugs.

"Are you thinking of staying here?" Nicholas asks.

"You can't stay here. What if they try to kill you again?" I cut in.

Owen exhales deeply.

"I don't know," he whispers under his breath.

The celebration is cut short, not by their incessant arguing but by the slow dawning of reality.

What do we do? Suddenly, the thoughts of flying to Paris first class and visiting Versailles and then having breakfast on a patio overlooking the Eiffel Tower vanish.

I want to bring them back.

I need to have them with me but these fantasies are quickly replaced with worries and the possibilities of what might happen if Owen were to get caught.

"I just feel like there's no way out," he says after a moment. "If I stay here, they're going to kill me. If I run, the cops are going to find me and send me back to prison."

The defeat on his face makes my heart break.

I reach over to him and wrap my arms around him.

He tilts his head down and places it softly on my shoulder.

"I don't know what to do either," I whisper into his ear.

27

OLIVE
WHEN WE ARE ALONE...

*W*ithout reaching much of a resolution or a decision, Owen leaves us to go to his room for the night.

I give him a brief hug and promise that nothing is going to happen to the painting.

I am sure that he still has his doubts but thankfully he keeps them to himself.

"Finally!" Nicholas says, his voice exploding in excitement.

Reaching into the minibar he pulls out a small bottle of tequila and a candy bar.

Leaning over the TV stand, he leafs through the little binder with the room service menu. "I'm starving," he adds, "but I didn't want to have dinner with him. No offense."

I shrug.

No offense taken but I still find his statement a bit rude.

"I hate this," I blurt out and immediately regret it.

"What's wrong?"

"I hate this...feud you two have. I wish you would be friends."

"I'm trying," he points out.

And I see it.

It's really mainly Owen who isn't trying very hard, yet I can't help but see his position.

Nicholas slept with his girlfriend and then she ended up dead.

He thinks he had something to do with it.

It's probably a miracle that every interaction they've had hasn't resulted in a full-blown fight.

"Yes, I know you are," I agree, putting my hand on his.

"You want me to try harder?" he asks, pulling himself a little closer.

I press my lips onto his, but when he opens his mouth, I put my head on his shoulder.

I want to kiss him but I want to feel better about this first.

"I have something that might cheer you up," Nicholas suddenly says, standing up and reaching behind the dresser.

A moment later he pulls out the Monet.

I stare at him unable to believe my eyes.

I look at him and then back at the painting and then back at him.

"How? Wait, but I was with you..." The words come out as fragments as I try to organize a coherent thought.

"You took it?" I finally ask.

He nods.

"But why?"

"Why else? It's worth a ton and it was there."

"Yes, of course." I shrug.

"Olive, frankly, I thought you would be a lot more excited about this," he says, propping the painting up against the wall.

I think I should be, too, but I'm also taken aback.

I thought that we would talk about it first.

And then something else occurs to me.

"Why didn't you show it to Owen when he was here?" I ask.

Nicholas turns away from me, ostensibly to fix the way the painting is leaning on the wall, but not really.

"Nicholas?" I press.

"Why do you think?" he asks, turning to face me.

He crosses his arms over his chest and withdraws somewhere far away.

"You're not planning on telling Owen?" I challenge him.

"I don't know what I'm planning to do but I didn't want to tell him then. I wanted to talk to you about it first."

This isn't a ridiculous notion but it still makes me angry.

"I just don't think you two will ever get along," I finally say.

"No kidding," he agrees. "But don't you see? He's the one who is making it so hard."

I do see that but I don't know what I'm supposed to do about it.

He's my brother. He's family and he needs my help.

But in order to help him, I need Nicholas' help.

"Where do you want to go?" I ask.

"With or without Owen?"

"Just...if it were up to you? Where would you go?"

He thinks about it for a moment. I wait. "Everywhere," he finally says. "Anywhere."

"That's not true," I say quietly. "You wouldn't go to...Ohio for instance."

He laughs.

"I would if you wanted to go to Ohio but I guess you're right, it wouldn't be my first choice."

"What would be your first choice?" I ask.

"I'd like to go to Europe with you, visit all the beautiful sights. But to live? California, I guess. We can visit LA and San Francisco but I'd like to settle down in some small town surrounded by mountains and bright blue skies that go on forever and palm trees."

Gazing into his eyes, I finally start to see my future.

Yes, of course.

This is what I wanted to hear.

This is where I can finally see us together as a family.

Happy and content.

"That sounds nice," I whisper. "It would be nice to get away from all of this cold and darkness. And I wouldn't say no to getting away from city life either."

"Good." He nods. "Then we can do that."

I plop onto the sofa and wave him over to me.

He sits down so close that our arms touch, sending shivers through me.

"I didn't mean anything by taking the Monet," he says quietly. "If you want to tell Owen about it, then do. I just wanted to give you the option."

I nod in agreement.

I understand.

Of course, I do.

And I believe him.

"I'm not upset by that," I say after a moment. "I just hate being in the middle so much. But I don't really have a choice. I don't know what the best thing to do is. If he stays here, they'll probably kill him. If he runs away, then he'll break parole and he'll be facing more years in prison."

Nicholas wraps his arm around my shoulder, pulling me closer to him.

When I look up, he puts his mouth on mine.

This time, I don't pull away.

This time, I turn toward him, burying my hands in his hair.

He lays me down onto the couch, draping his body over mine. Our mouths intertwine along with our tongues and we lose ourselves in the ebb and flow of our movements.

Somehow, my clothes end up on the floor along with his.

Somehow, we find ourselves on the bed.

The moments are both instantaneous and everlasting.

I want to be here with him forever and even an eternity is not enough.

Afterward, tired and spent, we fall asleep, our naked bodies still pressed against one another's.

28

NICHOLAS
WHEN I MEET WITH HIM...

*T*his time Art doesn't want to meet in our usual place, instead opting for a local mall.

I find him on a bench near the fake evergreen trees just a little bit over from the children's play area.

I listen to the kids' loud voices echo above their heads and watch their tired mothers stare at their phones for a brief reprieve from a day full of diaper changes, snack preparation, and meltdowns.

There's no narrow alleyway or a dark booth in a bar. It may be an unusual location for what we're about to do, but it's the ordinariness of this place that makes it above suspicion.

It's a little after two in the afternoon, and we are just two acquaintances running into each other at a mall.

Art shows up dressed in a pullover and slacks, the attire of a suburban husband. He's carrying three large paper shopping bags with the store's branding on the front.

Holding a hot dog, he takes a seat next to me and bites into it.

"You have it?" he asks, chewing with his mouth open.

I nod at my oversized Macy's bag and the tube sticking out of it like a French baguette.

I wait for him to look at it but he doesn't.

He simply continues to stare at a little boy struggling on the jungle gym.

"What now?" I ask after a few minutes.

"Now, we're done," he says slowly.

I'm not expecting payment.

My payment is that he loses my file and I no longer owe the FBI a thing.

I am certain he will pay this debt because the last thing he wants is for me to come out and tell his employers about this little exchange.

"So, we're good?" I ask to double check.

I let out a sigh of relief, even though I know it's premature.

"What are you going to do?" I ask.

I still don't like him and he still doesn't like me, but this job has somehow brought us closer to each other.

"I'm going to pay off my debt and hopefully put all of that behind me," he says.

I appreciate this moment of honesty.

"You need to disappear for a little while, if not for a long while. New passport, new identity, the works," Art says. "They'll look for you for a bit, but they got a few other sources in the organization so they shouldn't look for you for too long."

I rub my middle finger on the back of my index finger and stare at the grain along the seam of my jeans.

"Are you still after Owen?" I ask.

"Yes," Art says without missing a beat. "It would be in his best interest to get lost as well."

I point out that he's on parole but this doesn't faze Art even a little bit.

"New documents and a new location should go a long way to helping him start a new life. From what I heard, from my other source, is that he doesn't have much time left."

I want to ask him about a hundred more questions but he simply pulls the tube out of my bag, places it in his, and walks away.

I continue sitting on that bench, marveling at the inherent trust in our exchange.

That tube I delivered him can contain a fake or nothing at all.

But if that were the case then neither of us would get what we want.

When he disappears into the crowd, I wonder if I'll ever see him again and know that if I do then it won't be a good thing.

I sit on that bench for a long time trying to figure out my next move.

I have disappeared before but I have never disappeared with another person, let alone with two, one of whom hates my guts.

An orchestrated disappearance is a permanent vacation.

You go somewhere else, become someone else, and then have to live with that identity for a very long time.

The last time I disappeared, it was not a full-blown effort. I went to Hawaii where no one knew me and I could make new friends and assume a new life, but I didn't really start a new life. I kept my name and people who wanted to reach me still could.

This time, however, things are different. To run away for good means putting aside the man everyone knows me to be.

The thing about lies is that it's easier to lie when you are the only one telling it. When you lie, you tend to memorize certain things and then tell them in the exact same way every time.

But when you tell the truth, your words vary depending on the circumstance. It's not that you elaborate or add any untrue details, it's just that the tempo of the story changes each time.

The fact that I have to disappear with two other people, one of whom is almost my enemy, makes the whole situation even more complicated.

You can promise to stick to a story but to what degree will Olive and Owen really adhere to it?

And to what degree will they stray from it?

I don't know the answers to these questions any more than I know the answers to whether or not we will end up in California.

Now, there are three of us in on this and I am not sure how much Owen shares our interest in cloudless skies, blue water, jagged mountains, and towering palm trees.

Lost in my own thoughts, I don't see them walking up to me until it's too late.

29

OLIVE

WHEN WE SEE HIM…

I don't want to follow him.

I want to trust him, and I do.

But Owen says he's going to do it whether I come with him or not.

I don't have a choice.

I come in protest but with full certainty that we have nothing to worry about.

Nicholas might have lied to me about certain things but his actions have proven him be a reliable partner.

He would never do anything to hurt me.

That's why standing here over the railing and watching their meeting puts tears in my eyes.

It's Art Hedison, an FBI agent, who has investigated me before.

He didn't find any evidence but that didn't stop him from questioning me.

When Owen asks me why I'm crying, I can't bring myself to lie.

I'm too much in shock by what I am seeing.

How could Nicholas do this to me? How could he betray me like this?

My ears ring and the mall's cacophony of sounds all blend into one.

Owen tugs on my shirt a few times before I finally register a thing.

"Who is that?" he asks over and over again. "You have to tell me everything."

"His name is Art Hedison," I say slowly, my vision focusing in on the two strangers below.

I know both of their names, and I used to think I was in love with one of them.

"He's an FBI agent," I say. "He investigated the other paintings I stole."

"What other paintings?" Owen asks.

I look at him.

His eyes are wide with inquiry and his face is flushed.

He knows nothing about my old life because I thought it would be better that way.

But now, it hardly matters.

"That's why Nicholas wanted to work with me," I say as a matter of fact. "I knew how to break into safes and steal paintings and that's what we did."

"So, you knew about this?" Owen asks, his eyebrows raising almost all of the way up to the top of his forehead.

"I had *no* idea," I say quietly.

My words are slow and detached.

I'm here and yet I'm not.

The world is moving in slow motion and everything is happening to someone else.

"What is he doing?" Owen asks.

That question I do not have an answer to.

"We have to go. If the FBI knows about this then..." His words trail off.

I look down at the bench again.

Art and Nicholas talk without looking at each other.

From our vantage point one level up, we can see practically all of the way over to Macy's on one end and Nordstrom's on the other.

There are no other agents anywhere near them.

I look around at the faces and people gathering around him and us.

Most are shoppers coming in and out of stores. I focus on the ones who are stationary.

They are the ones who are likely undercover.

There are moms near the playground. Some are chatting with their friends, others have their heads buried in their phones.

There are two groups of teenagers gushing over each other's purchases.

And then there are the lone kiosk salespeople, waiting patiently for someone to walk by and give them attention.

Any of these people can be an undercover FBI agent.

I look closer for signs.

Are they talking into their wrists? Are they looking around a little bit too much?

No, surprisingly, they are not.

Owen keeps trying to tell me more and then he starts to tug on my shirt to get me to leave.

I brush him off both times and focus my attention on Nicholas.

After a few more words, Art moves the rolled up painting from Nicholas' bag to his and walks away.

I hold my breath.

This is when someone would charge at Nicholas.

Or at me. Or at Owen.

A moment later, I realize that I had shut my eyes.

I open them and wait.

Nicholas continues to sit on the bench.

Is he waiting for something? For someone?

More time passes.

Owen tries to pull me away again.

"We have to go," he whispers into my ear over and over.

But I wait.

If someone was going to arrest us, they would do it already.

The painting has been exchanged. Whatever deal Nicholas made with Art is complete.

But nothing happens.

Nicholas sits on the bench for close to twenty minutes before he finally gets up and walks back to his car.

"What the hell is going on?" I ask Owen, but he is just as bewildered as I am.

"Let's follow him," Owen says when we get to my car.

But I have a better idea.

I start the engine and drive straight to our hotel room.

Owen argues with me all the way over.

When Nicholas took off this morning, he left his stuff there including the Monet.

————

OWEN IS mad at me for letting Nicholas go, but I tune him out. As soon as we get to my hotel room, I want to go straight inside but unfortunately the housekeepers are right in the middle of their daily cleaning.

I tell them that I have a headache and ask if they mind cutting it short.

When they leave, I ask Owen to close the door and lock it. Walking over to the dresser below the mounted television, I hear my heart pound through my chest.

I reach my hand behind it and pull out the painting.

"What's that?" Owen asks, just as the door starts to open.

"It's the other painting we took from that house," I tell him. "It's a sketch that Monet made for one of his lilies. At least I think so."

The door creaks when it opens. Nicholas comes in.

"I guess you told him," he says quietly.

30

OLIVE

WHEN HE COMES OVER…

*T*he arrogant expression on his face makes me want to punch him.

Who the hell does he think he is coming here and acting like I am the one who is doing something wrong?

"Who did you give that painting to?" I blurt out.

His smile vanishes and his eyes narrow.

"Owen, will you give us a minute?" he asks, holding the door open with his hand.

Owen doesn't move from the sofa and just waits.

"No, he can stay," I answer for him.

"Owen, please."

"I want him to stay," I insist.

When I glance over, I see that Owen has no intention of leaving me alone.

"Okay, that's fine," Nicholas says after a moment.

His words are careful and methodical.

He takes a few more steps closer to me but stops about an arm's length away.

"What were you doing with *him*?" I burst.

My voice cracks up in the middle and lets out a big squeak, startling everyone in the room including me.

"That was my contact," he answers.

I shake my head and look down at the floor.

"How much money did you get?" Owen asks.

"I'll get it later," Nicholas says after a moment.

"When?"

"Soon." He nods vigorously.

There's an earnestness to him that might compel someone to believe what he's saying.

I'm lucky though. I know the truth.

"So, how much is it going to be?" I toy with him.

I want a number.

I want him to lie to me.

At this point, I am practically begging for it.

"I'd rather just tell you, Olive."

"I was there for the job, Nicholas. What's the big deal?" Owen asks.

He sits back in the sofa and crosses his legs with his ankle on his knee.

He doesn't respond.

There's tension in the air and I know he can sense it.

He must know that something is wrong.

"Can I talk to you?" he whispers under his breath. "Please?"

I let out a sigh and give Owen a nod.

He doesn't want to leave but I insist.

I need an explanation and I know that I won't get one with my brother here.

"I'll be right outside," Owen says.

"Go to your room," I say like a scolding mother.

"I'll be in the hallway," he says, closing the door behind him.

"Why did you show him the Monet?" Nicholas rushes over to me, taking me into his arms. "That was supposed to be our... secret. Our backup."

"Our backup in case of what?" I challenge him.

My eyes narrow and I cross my hands in front of my chest.

"In case things didn't work out with *him*," he whispers.

"Oh, yeah? And what is my backup plan in case things don't work out with *you*?"

He glares at me.

One blank stare follows another.

"I'm such an idiot," I say, rubbing my temples. "I'm such a moron!"

"What are you talking about?"

"Art Hedison." I say the name slowly, enunciating every syllable.

Blood drains away from his face.

"Yeah, you know who I'm talking about." I point my finger at him. "That's who you met with today. That's who has our painting."

"Olive—you don't understand," Nicholas starts to mutter.

"Why are you talking to the FBI?"

"I'm not."

I laugh, tossing my head back with a loud snort.

"I'm not," he says. "I mean, I am but I'm not. It's not what it looks like."

"Oh, yeah? 'Cause I have a pretty good idea from watching your little exchange today."

"He had me, Olive. They had a case on me and I had to be his informant to keep them from filing charges."

I listen and then nod for him to continue.

He takes a deep breath.

"And then Art got into some trouble. Bad gambling debts. And he asked me to steal that painting. In return, he'd lose my file. I wouldn't be an informant anymore. I'd be free."

I shake my head.

"You lied to me," I whisper.

"No, I didn't," he says, taking me into his arms.

I push him away but he doesn't let me go.

I could force him off me but for some reason I don't.

I hate him but I love him.

Even now.

Even after all that he has done.

"Who were you informing on?" I ask, looking up into his tear-filled eyes.

He looks away.

I wait.

He doesn't answer.

"Who were you informing on, Nicholas?" I ask again.

My heart starts to race.

At first, it was just a question that I thought would have some generic answer.

But now, looking at him, I know that things are a lot more complicated than I ever thought.

"Owen," Nicholas says quietly. "They wanted me to befriend him. Follow him. They have a case on him."

I shake my head.

When he pats my back, I push him away.

"No, no, no," I whimper.

Nicholas starts to explain but I can't make out his words through the blood rushing in between my temples.

All I know is that I want him to go away.

I don't want him touching me.

I don't want to ever see him again.

"You need to go," I force myself to say.

"Olive, please," Nicholas pleads. "Let me explain."

He launches into another explanation and I don't hear this one either.

Instead, I open the dresser drawer and grab all of his neatly folded clothes and toss them into his suitcase.

He tries to stop me but I manage to do the same thing with the second drawer.

That's when I see it.

Something bright peeks out through the clothes and catches my eye. When I rifle for it, I find a diamond bracelet, a diamond ring, and a diamond encrusted watch with the word Rolex on the face plate.

"What's this?" I ask.

"That's—" he starts to say.

"You took that from the house, didn't you?"

Nicholas nods.

"And you weren't going to tell me? Tell us?"

"I was going to tell you," he says.

"When?"

"You thought we were going to get paid for that painting," Nicholas explains. "I needed to take something and sell it. The Monet was our secret stash. This jewelry was going to be the money that we split with Owen."

"You." I point my finger in his face, trying to think of just the right thing to call him. "You're such a *liar!*"

We argue deep into the night but it only makes my resentment and anger worse.

The more he tries to explain, the less I want to listen.

The more I close off, the harder he tries to make things right.

We go in circles until we are both dizzy and exhausted, our relationship fracturing and breaking into more pieces with each word.

Finally, when I am too tired to keep going, I ask him to leave.

"I'm sorry, Olive. I'm sorry about everything."

"I'm sorry, too."

He zips up his suitcase with all of his clothes and then turns to me. "I'm going to take the jewelry and the watch but I want you to keep the Monet. I'm sorry I didn't tell you the truth but I just couldn't. It wasn't safe and I didn't want to put you in danger."

"Don't act like you were doing me any favors," I snap.

"It's all true. Please believe me," he tries again.

He puts his hands around my shoulders.

I shrug it away. "I have something for you. I was saving it for the right time but now I'm not sure we'll have one."

"I don't want anything from you," I snap.

"You want this," Nicholas insists and pulls a folder out of his suitcase. He lays it on the bed and leaves.

31

OLIVE
AFTERWARD…

*a*s soon as he leaves, I break down. My feet, as if frozen in place, refuse to cooperate and I simply crumble to the floor.

I wrap my arms around my shoulders and sob, holding nothing back.

Somewhere in the distance, I hear Owen's forceful knocks and pleas to let him in.

"Go away," I manage to utter through my tears.

I cry until my eyes dry out.

When I get inside the bathroom, I notice that my shirt is soaked at my wrists from wiping my cheeks. Mascara is smeared around my eyes.

I splash some water on my face and then collect it in my palms and bury my face in it.

It's cool and refreshing, pulling some of the heat away from my skin.

Wishing I could submerge my whole body in it, I turn on the faucet in the bathtub.

The rush of the water startles me for a second. I feel the temperature and then turn the knob to get it a bit warmer.

When the tub is filled almost to the top, I take off my clothes and climb in.

More tears come.

Instead of wiping them, I just tilt my head back and push myself under.

The water wraps itself around me. I want to stay here forever.

When I run out of breath, I bring my head up to the surface, just so that my nose and mouth are exposed.

I inhale deeply and disappear below again.

I do this over and over again until finally I start to feel better.

The pain in my chest subsides a bit and my heart doesn't feel like it's squeezed by some powerful force over and over again.

Sometime later, I get enough strength to climb out of the tub.

I dry myself with a towel, wrap my hair with another, and put on the bathrobe hanging on the back of the door.

It's thick and fluffy and it does its best to make me feel like maybe my life isn't a total wreck if only for a moment.

When my thoughts return to Nicholas and his betrayal, tears start to well up again but I stop them in their tracks.

No, I'm not going to think about this.

I need some time. In the meantime, I need to distract myself with something else. I pick up my phone and try to focus on a novel that I've been reading, but the words don't make any sense and I have trouble following the story.

I read the same page three times before I give up.

I need something stronger, something more distracting.

Turning on the television, I flip through the channels until I get to HGTV. A couple is buying a house in Costa Rica.

They seem to exist in a whole different world, if not on another dimension.

I turn it off when they start arguing about the size of the closets and the type of pool they want.

Sometimes, it's good to lose yourself in someone else's banal problems, but sometimes it just makes everything even more shitty.

I lie down on the bed and feel the coarseness of the bedspread under my fingertips.

The weave is thick and luxurious and I let my fingers follow one knot down to another and another. When I touch the folder, my fingers recoil but then immediately reach for it again.

I'm angry with him.

The exact intensity of it is difficult to describe.

Every cell within my body feels like it's about to explode. I trusted him and he betrayed me.

Maybe I'm a fool for thinking he wouldn't lie to me.

Maybe this whole thing was a con from the beginning.

Maybe nothing he ever told me was true.

Memories of everything we have been through run through my mind in circles.

Nothing is in order, and every memory sparks in a flash and then fades just as fast.

Was everything that happened a lie or was it mostly the truth with just a peppering of the untrue?

Or was it another way around altogether?

Mostly a lie with just a few kernels of truth?

I thought I knew that he loved me.

A part of me thought he didn't tell me because of the same reason I couldn't say it to him.

But now, I'm wondering whether he didn't bother saying it because it would be yet another lie.

I touch the folder again.

It's smooth and soft, the exact opposite of the jaggedness that is my life.

Nicholas said he was waiting for the right time to give it to me.

I have no idea what's in it and I am tempted to just throw it in the trash.

I don't want anything from him, not anymore.

Not after what he has done to me.

Still, I can't bring myself to toss it.

Whatever is in here, it has to be somewhat important or he wouldn't have bothered giving it to me.

Do I dare to open it?

The folder is a creamy manila type with worn edges and signs of wear.

Sitting up on the edge of the bed and tapping my foot on the floor, I slowly open the first page.

On top, I find a handwritten note addressed to Nicholas.

THIS IS everything I managed to find about Olive Kernes' real mother.

.   .   .

My heart jumps into my throat and my hands begin to shake.

The next page contains the DNA results, showing that there is a 99.9% chance that a woman named Josephine Rose Reyes is her.

My hands begin to shake so hard I worry that I'm going to drop the folder onto the floor.

I lay it carefully on the bed and wait for my heart rate to slow down before looking at the rest of the documents.

"When did you do this?" I ask Nicholas as if he were in the room.

A part of me wishes he were here so that he could hold me in his arms as I look through this.

"And why didn't you tell me sooner? Why... why did you have to lie?" I whimper and reach for the next page.

LEAVING HOME

February 1994

32

*J*osephine, who told everyone to call her Joey, opened the road atlas that she bought at a gas station and tried to figure out how to read it.

She'd just gotten her driver's license but she had never opened a map before.

How were you supposed to know where you were in order to figure out which road to take to go where you were going?

She had no definite idea where she planned on going except that she needed to get away from her parents' house as soon as possible.

She had been to a great many places, ocean

beach houses, the ski slopes, rambling mansions in the middle of nowhere, and sprawling penthouses overlooking major cities.

But it was always her parents or the driver who had taken her there. This time, she was going alone and no one could know where she was headed.

Joey bought her used 1985 Datsun with her own money under an assumed name.

The guy who advertised it in the Pennysaver was a father of four who was reluctant to sell it to a seventeen-year-old girl with the look of a deer in the headlights.

But when she offered him two hundred dollars over asking price and he thought about his kids who were currently living in an apartment with no heat, he couldn't resist.

Buying this car depleted most of her savings, leaving her with about two thousand dollars in cash.

She had a credit card that she could use, of course, but her parents would trace that immediately so if she wanted to stay hidden that was off limits. Two grand would have to be enough to start a new life for her and her baby. But how that was all going to happen, she wasn't sure yet.

Josephine Rose was the youngest daughter of Mr. and Mrs. Reyes. On the surface, she grew up with everything a little girl could ever want. A large apartment on Park Avenue with her own room, an ensuite bathroom, and a devoted mother who indulged her interest in dolls and dressing up. In their house in the Hamptons, she also had a separate playroom and a treehouse where she could let her imagination run wild.

Mr. and Mrs. Reyes employed a chef, a housekeeper, and a nanny who helped Mrs. Reyes run the rather extensive household as well as host all of their dinner parties and events.

Josephine attended the best private schools where she became friends with the children of other prominent citizens of New York. Though her life wasn't entirely planned out, there were certain things that were expected of her.

She was expected to attend an exclusive university, to get a job or an internship in her chosen profession after graduation, and eventually meet and marry a man from a similarly well-established family.

What her parents did not expect, or even consider a possibility, was that on the night of her debutante ball, their daughter would tell them that she was pregnant and wanted to keep the child.

Zipping her big belly into an oversized sweatshirt, Joey climbed behind the wheel.

She started her journey on purpose in the afternoon because the mornings never treated her well. The Datsun was parked in a public parking spot not too far away from her parents' apartment and sitting down behind the wheel for the first time yesterday filled her with a sense of freedom she hadn't felt since she was a little girl.

It took forever to get out of New York City in all of the traffic and she only made it as far as Pennsylvania. But that was okay. She still needed to figure out where she was going.

North was out of the question because she hated the cold.

South would be the easiest because Florida was relatively cheap and warm this time of year.

She had been there a number of times to their condo in Miami but she had no interest in going to any city where her father had any ties. Still, Florida was a big state, full of little towns she could get lost in. It was definitely a possibility.

But so was something else. California.

It was stupid and ridiculous to drive across the whole country all by herself but her heart continued to call her westward.

How did that saying go again?

*The West is the best. Come here and we'll do the
rest.*

She was already doing something ludicrous
and stupid, so why not take it all the way to
the Pacific Ocean?

For all of their travels to Europe, Asia, and
Mexico, Mr. and Mrs. Reyes had never taken
their children to California. And that was
precisely why their youngest child chose this
as her destination on that dreary and cold
Pennsylvania afternoon.

With the gas tank full, and her passenger seat
full of her favorite snacks, Joey started the
engine and headed west on the turnpike
going east.

She opened a pack of peanut M&M's and
turned up the sound on the radio.

Nirvana was playing in heavy rotation and
she sang along at the top of her lungs
watching the videos that she had seen a
million times in her mind.

It had been dark for hours when she pulled into a motel right near the outskirts of Pittsburgh and paid cash for the room.

The woman at the counter suspected that she was well under eighteen but taking one look at her belly and her bags, she decided to not risk scaring her off by asking for identification. She had been a kid just like her only a few decades before. Pregnant, scared, all alone, and running away from her mother's abusive boyfriend.

Once inside, Joey propped her feet up on one of the double beds and fell into a deep blissful sleep.

She didn't stir again until four that morning when nausea rushing up from the pit of her stomach stirred her awake.

Not quite making it all the way to the toilet, Joey threw up some of the bile into her open hands.

33

Joey spent most of the morning until checkout time in bed, trying to summon the strength to get into the car.

The hardest thing was not so much driving but forcing herself to her feet, packing up the few things that she took out of her bag, having some food and finally dragging everything, including herself, to the parking lot.

Besides throwing up every morning and feeling nauseous most of the day especially if she stood on her feet too long, this baby growing inside of her made her feel very lethargic.

Even the most basic things like brushing her teeth or her hair took a considerable amount of coaxing and convincing while she lay in bed staring at her paperbacks.

Joey had always loved to read.

Ever since she was a little girl and the nanny read her first books to her, she had been enthralled by the words found there.

These worlds were so much like the one that she lived in and yet they were also so different.

One of her favorites was called the *True Confessions of Charlotte Doyle*. It was about a thirteen-year-old girl from a well-to-do family in the 1830s who travels from England to America to meet her family. There were supposed to be other people coming with her but she ended up being the only woman on a working ship run by a cruel captain.

What Joey liked so much about this book was that unlike other books about women in the nineteenth century, Charlotte was a very modern girl.

She started out afraid and timid but through her journey she evolved and started sympathizing with the crew over the awful captain. And the end? That was her favorite part of the story! Charlotte rejected her stuffy upbringing and her confining family to live a life of adventure on the high seas.

Joey Rose saw herself as a contemporary Charlotte Doyle. She may not have been on a ship, but she was fighting against her upbringing.

She was starting a new life on her own terms. She would make her own money.

She would make her own decisions. She would raise her child according to her own rules, not the ones set out by her parents.

Joey re-read her favorite parts of the book and then rifled through the stack of a few others that she'd brought along for the trip.

Her books made up the majority of her luggage and she wouldn't have it any other way.

It was fifteen minutes until checkout and she couldn't wait any longer.

Joey slowly got out of bed and went to the bathroom. She brushed her hair and put on a little bit of makeup to give her face some color.

She'd washed her hair the night before and slept on it wet. Strands near the crown of her head were sticking out in different directions and no amount of brushing put them in place.

She pushed them down with water and then pulled her hair into a bun.

This would just have to do, she decided.

After packing up her makeup and her books and changing into a pair of oversized jeans and the same long sleeve t-shirt she'd worn for the last few days, she grabbed her bag, zipped up her hoodie, and climbed into the car.

The hours on the road passed quickly. She hadn't had her license for long but there was nothing like a cross-country road trip to really make you comfortable behind the wheel.

By the time she drove out of Missouri and into Oklahoma, she was no longer nervous at pulling out a tape from the tape deck, popping it into the plastic folder, and putting in another one.

She had been devouring a new book on tape she'd gotten from the New York Public Library - it was about a woman in 1940s Britain who found herself back in 1700s Scotland.

It was called *Outlander* and Joey found the language and the love story between Jamie and Claire utterly delicious.

Actually, the book meant even more than that. It gave her hope for her own life, only the way that books could.

She, too, was traveling into the unknown.

She, too, found herself in a world that was very foreign to her.

But if Claire could make it out alright then she would as well, right?

In the northeastern part of Oklahoma, Joey let out a sigh of relief. The sky was wide and blue and the land was immense.

If it weren't for a few other passengers who traveled on the interstate along with her, she would be completely alone.

And though the nature was clearly tamed by man and their tractors and tools, she could feel that real freedom was not that far away.

The natural world was calling her and the farther west she got, the freer she felt.

Joey wasn't sure if it was the lack of the tall buildings, the lack of the millions of people crammed into one five-mile island, or just the thousand miles that now separated her from her parents that made her feel invincible.

Or maybe it was just a combination of all of those things.

In any case, after all of this travel, she was finally starting to feel like she might get away with it. Little did she know that there was a search party already looking for her.

Joey thought that during her parents' trip to Paris would be the perfect time to disappear.

She could still call them there from the road and pretend like she was at home, giving herself three days of a head start.

What she did not know, and could not have a way of knowing, was that her mom came home early one day from the spa and discovered her dad in bed with his long-time girlfriend, a student at Sorbonne.

Mrs. Reyes cut the trip short, came home early, and discovered that her daughter was gone.

The housekeeper folded under scrutiny from the private investigator.

Joey suspected that she would but she couldn't *not* tell her where she was going because then she would've notified her parents even earlier. Luckily, she only told her the bare minimum and threw in a few lies about going to Canada to get them off her scent.

34

*M*r. and Mrs. Reyes had been unhappily married for too many years but the thing that always kept them together was their children.

There were four and Josephine, as they preferred to call her, was the youngest.

As far as they were concerned, their other children did everything that was expected of them.

They played sports, excelled in extracurricular activities, and rarely talked back to them.

Whenever they spoke of their kids at parties,

their friends who were going through many normal hard patches of raising teenagers were jealous of them.

What they did not know, however, was that like their parents, the Reyes children were very good at living double lives.

Their oldest son was a star athlete in his prep school and then at Harvard but in between applying to law schools, he became one of the biggest dealers of ecstasy and cocaine across the Ivy Leagues.

Their second-oldest, also a son, was one of his first customers and a full-blown addict who still managed to maintain a B-average at Dartmouth.

Their eldest daughter, the president of her class, an Olympic hopeful in skiing, had her sights on Yale medical school.

She had also struggled with bulimia and anorexia since she was eleven and popped anti-depressants and sleeping pills like they were candy.

Neither of the two parents knew anything about their children's double lives.

Not because the kids were particularly good at deception but rather that they didn't really want to look at them too closely.

Joey knew all of this and hated the hypocrisy that was her everyday existence.

On the outside, her family was picture perfect, All-Americans down to the blonde hair and sun-kissed skin.

But brewing just below was a torrent of anger, disappointment, and resentments that had been building up over a lifetime.

Her three older siblings were always a team that were as impenetrable as her parents.

There was a time when she wanted to be close to her sister but she always considered Joey an annoyance if not a pest. And so, Joey got used to being alone and keeping to herself.

Then Danny showed up.

Danny Lebold did not belong at Bloomfield, or at least that was what everyone said whenever they whispered his name.

His mother was a nurse who worked double shifts to pay his tuition. He had wanted to go to the private school as much as his mother wanted to send him there and worked his butt off trying to get the best grades he could. Back in his large, overcrowded high school, Danny got straight A's and got angry whenever he received anything less than an A-. But at Bloomfield, he struggled.

There were no spots during his ninth grade year, so he transferred in the middle of his tenth when a student got expelled for driving the head of the school's car into the lake while intoxicated. His parents, of course, fought the expulsion but this was not that student's first offense so their lawyers managed to convince them to let it go.

Thus, Bloomfield had an opening for Danny and he jumped at the chance. But coming into the school year in the middle was a special kind of hell.

Not only had most of the kids known each other since pre-school, the education at his public school was nowhere near as rigorous as it was there.

The year before, they had another transfer. That kid had the personality of a political candidate on the campaign trail so he quickly became the most popular guy on campus. But Danny was shy and quiet and not very good at small talk and that was why the only person at Bloomfield who immediately took a liking to him was Josephine Reyes.

When Joey first approached Danny, he was sitting in the corner of the lunchroom with his head buried in the *Lord of the Rings*.

She had never read that book herself but that didn't stop her from taking the seat next to him and introducing herself.

She had never been particularly outgoing, but something about this new kid gave her the strength to overcome her timidness.

He was tall and dark with beautiful green eyes. He was also quite attractive even though he didn't seem to know this at all.

They talked about classes (Mrs. Matusiak gave the worst pop quizzes) and sports (neither of them were big fans of playing or watching) and movies (they had both loved *Jurassic Park* and *the Firm* and Joey was looking forward to seeing *Interview with the Vampire*).

She had read the book in preparation just like she always did but she was not one of those people who automatically thought the book was better than the movie.

To her, the movie was an entirely different medium so she never expected to see the whole book unfold line by line on screen.

If they had managed to capture even a little bit of the theme and the tone of the book and ended up making a good movie, she was satisfied.

Danny, on the other hand, wasn't. To him, no movie ever lived up to how it was in his head and on the page and that left him forever frustrated and annoyed with any film adaptation.

Joey and Danny quarreled about a great many things over their first year of friendship but none of the fights were taken seriously by either side.

They were more like oral arguments, each one trying to convince the other that they were right.

And it was in one of those moments that they each realized how much the other person really meant to them.

The first time Joey and Danny kissed, he had met her near her locker, said something funny that made her snort, and then pressed his lips to hers.

She continued laughing for a few moments before she realized what had happened and then she threw her arms around his neck and pushed her tongue down his throat.

Joey had a crush on Danny since the first day they met.

She wanted to ask him out right there and then but this was high school and she was too shy and inexperienced and thought that becoming friends would make it easier.

Little did she know that it would actually complicate the matter.

Danny had liked her since before she even said hi to him. He had seen her around school and he liked her quiet way of being. He also liked her dark eyeshadow and the fact that she drew stars in blue pen on her sneakers.

But the closer that they became as friends, the harder it was for him to make a move.

What if she wasn't interested in him like that?

What then?

Would their friendship survive his crush?

Danny decided to wait, either for his fear to subside or his courage to multiply.

And then one moment when she was laughing hysterically, with her hair falling into her face and her eyes closed, he just went for it.

He'd tried to do this before but his fear had always stopped him.

Not this time.

This time, he just took a step closer to her and let his mouth do the rest.

35

When Joey got into New Mexico, that was the first time that she had seen the purple mountain majesty.

The hills surrounded the road on both sides, rising high and almost kissing the impossibly blue sky.

The earth was reddish brown, to match the setting sun and the views took her breath away.

Driving through Albuquerque, she fell in love with the salmon-colored highway and the turquoise blue overpasses.

The cloudless sky that allowed the sun to shine brightly lifted whatever worries she was carrying. It was almost as though she had left everything in her past somewhere out east and she could start her life over out here.

When she got to Phoenix and saw her first saguaro cactus towering over the desert floor with its thick round branches reaching up to the heavens, she pulled the car over for a closer look.

Examining its delicate fruit and the protective spines, she decided that from now on she would never be Josephine Rose Reyes again.

Her new name would Joey Lebold and if she didn't like California then she would come back to Arizona and live there.

The baby kicked and she placed her hand on top of her belly and told her of her plans out loud, so that she would hear.

This seemed to soothe her because the kicking stopped and she moved so that she wouldn't be pressing up so hard against Joey's esophagus, giving her heartburn.

If only Danny were here, she thought and wiped away a tear. She couldn't think about him too much because that was when the waterworks would start.

Unfortunately, the tears were not just due to the hormones. Danny was supposed to be there. They were supposed to be taking this trip and starting their lives together.

And if it weren't for that accident then they would be.

When they first found out that she was pregnant, they were terrified. They had used protection but one time the condom broke and she couldn't get the morning-after pill without a prescription and she couldn't get a prescription without going to the doctor.

She couldn't go to the doctor without her parents finding out.

So, they just prayed that it would turn out okay.

Of course, it didn't.

And after?

She wasn't sure what to do or what she even wanted to do.

Danny was as scared as she was so they did what teenagers often do, waited until the problem went away.

Only, it didn't go away.

Her stomach kept getting bigger and after a while their decision was made for them.

That was when Danny asked her to marry him.

She said yes and he put a ring on her finger.

That was before they told his mom who kicked them both out of the house. That was before they told her parents who forced her to remove the ring from her finger, called their family physician for an emergency house call, and kicked Danny out of the house.

Her parents insisted on an abortion and forbid her from ever seeing Danny again.

His mom told him she hadn't worked her butt off her whole life providing for a kid who would throw his whole future away on some trashy girl.

She said that the only way she would permit him back into her house was if he dumped Joey and never saw the baby.

That was when Danny and Joey made their own plans.

They were going to run away together.

They were going to get married in Vegas and they were going to start their lives away from their awful parents who didn't understand a thing about love or family.

They were going to sneak out in the middle of the night and drive Danny's car for hours to get as far away from there as possible.

But when Joey waited out on the curb with her bags, Danny didn't show up.

She waited for hours and then finally called his house around eight that morning.

His mother picked up.

She was sobbing and Joey could barely make out a thing she was saying.

Later that morning, she learned that Danny was dead.

He had died, earlier that night, in a car accident when someone rear-ended him and pushed him into traffic.

Later, after the funeral, a police officer took Joey aside and, after a few questions, revealed that Danny had two suitcases with him with everything he owned in the world.

He had not stood her up.

He had died on his way to running away with her.

That was when Joey made the decision to not stand him up either.

Two weeks later, she put their plan into action and three weeks later, she saw the sign welcoming her into California.

36

NICHOLAS
AFTERWARD...

I walk out of the hotel a broken man.

I wanted more time to explain but deep down what I really wanted was more time to convince her that I didn't betray her.

But would more time make her understand?

What exactly am I trying to convince her of?

That somehow I didn't meet with an FBI agent and report to him on her brother?

That we didn't steal that painting in order to help me, not us?

I have told her too many lies.

They have finally caught up with me and because I never told her I love her, now she'll never know the truth.

I get into my car and start driving.

I don't know where, but it feels good to just be going.

Besides Olive I don't need anything else here.

I can get my fake identification sent to me wherever I am.

No one is looking for me yet, and I have some time.

Maybe I have too much time and too many options.

I watch the white abbreviated lines between the lanes disappear under my car.

The world becomes a blur, but I keep driving.

Where do I go now?

Where do I go from here?

Will we ever see each other again?

***

Thank you for reading TELL ME TO RUN!

I hope you enjoyed continuing Nicholas and Olive's story. Can't wait to find out what happens next?

One-click TELL ME TO FIGHT now!

 I'm a man who takes what he wants.

What do I want? Her.

Olive Kernes owned me a debt and she thought that she had paid it back.

But now I want more.

I want more than just her time.

I want more than just her body.

Her new life has torn us apart.

Now, it's up to me to make things right.

I will make the pieces of our love fit back together if it's the last thing I do.

But can I do it in time?

Dive into the dangerous 5th book of the new and addictive TELL ME series by bestselling author Charlotte Byrd.

One-click TELL ME TO FIGHT now!

————

I APPRECIATE you sharing my books and telling your friends about them. Reviews help readers find my books! Please leave a review on your favorite site.

CONNECT WITH CHARLOTTE BYRD

S ign up for my **newsletter** to find out when I have new books!

You can also join my Facebook group, **Charlotte Byrd's Reader Club,** for exclusive giveaways and sneak peaks of future books.

I appreciate you sharing my books and telling your friends about them. Reviews help readers find my books! Please leave a review on your favorite site.

SIGN UP FOR THE VIP READER LIST

VIP Readers get new release updates, bonus content, and exclusive giveaways!

SIGN UP NOW!

ALSO BY CHARLOTTE BYRD

All books are available at ALL major retailers! If you can't find it, please email me at charlotte@charlotte-byrd.com

The Perfect Stranger Series
The Perfect Stranger
The Perfect Cover
The Perfect Lie
The Perfect Life
The Perfect Getaway

All the Lies Series
All the Lies
All the Secrets
All the Doubts

Tell me Series

Tell Me to Stop

Tell Me to Go

Tell Me to Stay

Tell Me to Run

Tell Me to Fight

Tell Me to Lie

Wedlocked Trilogy

Dangerous Engagement

Lethal Wedding

Fatal Wedding

Tangled Series

Tangled up in Ice

Tangled up in Pain

Tangled up in Lace

Tangled up in Hate

Tangled up in Love

Black Series

Black Edge

Black Rules

Black Bounds

Black Contract

Black Limit

Not into you Duet

Not into you

Still not into you

Lavish Trilogy

Lavish Lies

Lavish Betrayal

Lavish Obsession

Standalone Novels

Dressing Mr. Dalton

Debt

Offer

Unknown

WANT TO BE THE FIRST TO KNOW ABOUT MY UPCOMING SALES, NEW RELEASES AND EXCLUSIVE GIVEAWAYS?

Sign up for my newsletter: https://www.subscribepage.com/byrdVIPList

Join my Facebook Group: https://www.facebook.com/groups/276400079439433/

Bonus Points: Follow me on BookBub and Goodreads!

ABOUT CHARLOTTE BYRD

Charlotte Byrd is the bestselling author of romantic suspense novels. She has sold over 1 Million books and has been translated into five languages.

She lives near Palm Springs, California with her husband, son, a toy Australian Shepherd and a Ragdoll cat. Charlotte is addicted to books and Netflix and she loves hot weather and crystal blue water.

Write her here:

charlotte@charlotte-byrd.com

Check out her books here:

www.charlotte-byrd.com

Connect with her here:

www.facebook.com/charlottebyrdbooks

www.instagram.com/charlottebyrdbooks

www.twitter.com/byrdauthor

Sign up for my newsletter: https://www.
subscribepage.com/byrdVIPList

Join my Facebook Group: https://www.
facebook.com/groups/276340079439433/

Bonus Points: Follow me on BookBub and
Goodreads!

facebook.com/charlottebyrdbooks

twitter.com/byrdauthor

instagram.com/charlottebyrdbooks

bookbub.com/profile/charlotte-byrd

Made in United States
North Haven, CT
11 September 2024

57245316R00211